Changers

By

Rob G Lerner

Wisdom arrives sooner to some than to others,
and not at all to those left at the lake.

Cover by PJ Hines

Summary

Changers

By
Rob G Lerner

Cover by PJ Hines

The death of Iowa's father reveals an amazing gift. Iowa's mother warns the teenager to guard the gift carefully, making her promise not to tell anyone. But when her mother unexpectedly dies and she is left without guidance, Iowa reveals the secret to a group of her closest friends. What follows is a combination of excitement and tragedy that will challenge an entire community to make things right. *Changers* is not simply a story about growing up. It is also a story about trust, survival, and what it means to be human. Readers of all ages will find something in *Changers* that will challenge their understanding of love and friendship.

Pomanjer Publishing Co., LLC

Published October 18, 2013

Copyright

Changers

Text copyright 2013 by Rob G. Lerner. Illustrations and cover copyright by PJ Hines.

About Pomanjer Publishing Co., LLC

Pomanjer Publishing Co., LLC, publishes fiction and non-fiction books that speak to our hearts and catch our idiosyncratic attention.

Contact information:

Email:
PomanjerPublishing@cox.net

Mail:
Pomanjer Publishing Co. LLC
PO Box 986, Vienna VA 22183

About the author, Rob G. Lerner

Rob G Lerner, tempered in the western states, resides in Virginia with his wife and son, whose favorite bird is a great blue heron that frequents the nearby creek. Rob, a wannabe Formula One race car driver and avid armchair mountain climber, has been crafting fiction for years. Follow his literary progress at his web site http://RobGLerner.com. Curious comments, questions, concerns can be sent to him by email or postal mail through the publisher, Pomanjer Publishing Co., LLC.

Previously by Rob G Lerner

The Boy Who Loved Dolphins
Published in 2012 as a Kindle e-book (111 pages): Timmy is a young boy who feels alienated from his mother and stepfather. He gravitates toward his aging and beloved grandfather, who fills his head with wild fantasies of life beneath the sea. When his grandfather suddenly dies, Timmy feels adrift, and when his family takes a vacation on the North Carolina coast, he tries to remain close to his grandfather by living out some of the old man's fantasies. Things take a strange turn when Timmy turns into a dolphin, and a group of wild dolphins adopt him. Ocean life should be as wonderful as his grandfather promised, but Timmy quickly realizes that fantasies are a poor substitute for family, friends, or his grandfather.

Dedication

To Alex

Changers

Table of Contents

Changers

Chapter One - Iowa's father was seriously ill this time.

Iowa's father was seriously ill this time. He had been ill for a number of weeks, often languishing in bed alone in a room at the back of the house that was set up to accommodate his strange, unknown illnesses. Iowa's mother said that it was different this time – it was more intense and likely to be his last – but Iowa could not remember a time when her father was not seriously ill, either lying in bed or spending days, sometimes weeks, away from home getting strange, unknown treatments. The treatments never worked, because when they were over and he was home, he would have a relapse sooner or later and either take to his bed or leave home for special help.

Iowa loved her father, and she feared the worst every time he became ill, and she would promise the universe or whatever that if he recovered this one time, she would be a better person, do better in school, or even be kind to her mother. Now, as she sat in her room, waiting for permission to see her father while her mother attended to the sick man in his own room, Iowa tried to remember all the things that she and Daddy, as she called him, had done together, all the things that had made their relationship so special.

But no matter how hard she tried, she couldn't come up with a single instance in which she and Daddy had done something that was in the least bit memorable. Certainly, they had done things together, but none of these things seemed special, none of them matched either the things other children did with their fathers or the stories they told about the great times they had with their fathers. In fact, the only things Iowa could recall with any clarity – and this after having lived with him for all her life – was his kind smile, the softness of his hands when they wiped the tears off her cheeks, or the sound of his voice when he spoke to her. Iowa couldn't remember a single time in which the man had raised his voice or had spoken to her in a way that was different than his normal, calm, measured manner of speaking. Perhaps he had scolded her once or twice, but his way of scolding was to highlight her error and then, smiling wanly, explain to her what she needed to do to rectify the problem. There were other times when he was clearly angry -- he would lower his head, raise his eyebrows, tighten his lips, and, looking over the tops of his black-framed glasses, stare at her until she understood that she had done something that met with his disapproval. Interestingly, that was all it took – a mere glance – and Iowa would crumble, ask forgiveness, and promise never again to do whatever it was that she had done. But despite these vague recollections, Iowa was uncertain whether she could retain enough of her Daddy after he passed away to be able to say that she had had a father like everyone else. Was it really possible that such paltry memories could survive when he was no longer with her?

However, there was one thing associated with her father's current state that didn't make sense. If he was as sick as her mother claimed, if this was going to be the last time that anyone would see him, then why didn't the woman call a doctor or take him to the hospital, or drive him to one of those places that never seemed to cure what ailed him? Iowa had asked her mother these very questions – several times, in fact – but her mother would only smile condescendingly and say that medical treatment was useless now and, when Iowa protested, that Iowa would understand when she was older. Older? How old would she have to be to understand that doctors and hospitals can't cure people like her father, or that there comes a point when people should be left alone to die quietly in their bedrooms? It was hard to believe that she would ever reach that age.

Iowa had been waiting in her room for about an hour. The lights had been off for most of the morning, although the curtains in her room were open and giant beams of golden sunlight poured through the window and illuminated everything with a golden, hopeful glow. Surrounded by her stuffed animals, pictures of faraway places, numerous books on white swans, and a life-sized, stuffed white swan – a gift from her father, she told her friends, although she knew it came from her mother, who had somehow managed to send it to her while her father was away from home seeking treatment – Iowa had been expecting her mother to come in any moment and solemnly inform her that all was well…at least for now. While she waited, she paged through a couple of her swan books, traced the outlines of the birds in the book with her right index finger, copied the same outlines with the same finger into the folds of her needlework bedspread, and mentally inventoried all the shapes and shadows in her room that looked vaguely like wild birds. What else was there to do? Iowa had nearly completed this inventory when she noticed, on a small table against the far wall of her room, a small, round, nondescript object covered with black splotches.

Iowa's eyesight had never been good – she wore pink-rimmed glasses, the lenses of which changed color according to the surrounding light, but she hated wearing them because she didn't like pink or the comments some of her classmates made when she put them on to see the board – and for a few moments she couldn't make heads or tails of the object, or understand why it was situated on the white cloth that covered the small table. Stretching across her bed (she didn't feel like getting up and walking over to the table) to take a closer look, she quickly recognized the splotches and understood why it occupied a privileged place on the table. Iowa picked up the object, which was a baseball-sized rock, and tossing it lightly up and down in her hand so that she could see each splotch, she observed the names of her closest friends, who had signed the rock and given it to her as a birthday present three years ago. It was unbelievable that she didn't immediately recognize the rock, because it came from the lake and these friends were as close to her – closer, in fact – as her own mother, maybe even her father. More than that, she considered these four friends her true family, a group to which her mother didn't belong.

"Iowa," her mother whispered, as she opened the girl's door and looked across the room at her only child. "Please come with me. I need to talk to you about your father." Iowa felt certain that she knew what her mother was going to say, and so it seemed silly and insincere to act as if one couldn't speak normally in these circumstances. Her father was dying this time – maybe he was already dead – and her mother simply wanted to explain the obvious and ask her to come to the man's room – her Daddy's room -- to pay her final respects. It wasn't a big secret, and it was embarrassing to watch her mother to create an aura of mystery and solemnity around something that a child half her age could have grasped in an instant. But despite her dislike of what she considered a silly charade, Iowa got up without a word and followed her mother down the hallway to her father's room, where they stopped and sat down in a couple of black beanbag chairs positioned just outside the door where her father was taking his last gasps of earthly air.

"Your Daddy…," her mother started to say but then stopped, because she was having difficulty looking at her daughter and articulating the words that she needed to say.

"I know, mother. He's dying."

There was a pause before her mother responded. "Yes," she said quietly, "but there's something else you need to know."

"I don't need to know anything. Daddy's dying, and there's not a thing that anyone can do about it." Against her will, tears began to flow down her cheeks, and her voice suddenly sounded deep and husky, quite unlike her normally firm, confident tone. She wanted to sound strong and uninvolved (she didn't want her mother to think she was weak and needed anyone's help), but she couldn't completely control her emotions, and it was all she could do to keep from breaking down completely in front of her mother.

"There's something else…," the woman started to say while reaching over to Iowa, who pulled away as if she couldn't bear her mother's touch. "Okay," she began again, this time with a determination to get everything out before it was too late. "We may only have a few minutes. There's something about your father you need to understand…"

"I don't need to understand anything."

"Yes, you need to understand this, and I am sorry I don't know how to explain it better. Your father is…well, he is what we call a changer. He has the ability to transform…change is probably a better word…to turn himself into an animal. I suppose that's better. But this has always been his problem, because long ago he lost the ability to control his animal nature…this is why all those trips, all those times he was so sick. I warned him, and he didn't listen. The pull was too great until it took over his will to…well, it's happening off and on and…and…"

"I don't understand. You're not making sense," Iowa said hotly, her voice having abruptly lost its unnatural, husky sound. Iowa felt certain that her mother was treating her like a child to explain something that she had both the intelligence and maturity to understand.

He mother closed her eyes and, breathing deeply, shook her head briefly, as if she were denying Iowa some unusual or unreasonable request. Suddenly opening her eyes and looking directly into Iowa's eyes, she told Iowa to stand up. "I want you to come with me," she said, grasping Iowa's hand and leading her into the man's room.

Iowa allowed herself to be taken into father's room, although she closed her eyes upon entering because she couldn't bear to see death hovering over his body and dancing around his bed. She kept them closed until her mother ceased pulling her hand and allowed it to drop, which signaled that she was standing beside his bed. Before she opened her eyes, however, Iowa was struck by the odd smell that filled her nose and permeated the room. The smell was not entirely unpleasant, but it was not her father's smell or the smell that often characterized their household, especially late at night after everyone was in bed. It was different, unexpected, and inexplicable. Iowa would not have been surprised if the room had smelled like death -- like a hospital room in which a man lies gasping for breath, tubes in his nose and mouth and medicines on small tables near his bed – but this was nothing like a hospital room or any other place in her experience where someone was sick. If she hadn't known better, she would have sworn that the room had an animal-like smell to it –it smelled like birds – and when she finally opened her eyes, she half-expected to be in a zoo, not in her father's room in her house. Iowa completely forgot the smell the second she saw her father.

The sick man was lying in his bed, his head propped up by three or four large, fluffy pillows (one of which must have been punctured, because there were white feathers around the pillow and scattered on tops of the blankets), while the rest of him, up to his neck, was covered by a slightly-yellowish sheet that looked remarkably twisted and rumpled. Iowa didn't know her father's age – he was old, certainly, but no older than the fathers of her friends – and yet the man under the covers looked ancient, as if he were over a hundred years old. His skin had yellowish cast to it, and he appeared to have lost so much weight that it outlined the bones in his head and made his dark eyes bulge out from his face. Although his eyes clearly followed her movements, the rest of him remained motionless, as if he were a mummy and not a still living, breathing being.

"Daddy," Iowa cried. She hesitated only for a moment before dropping to her knees, pressing her cheek to the man's side, and stroking his claw-like, emaciated hand. Her father didn't move, however, and as she continued to softly call his name, she began to notice that there was something peculiar about him, something every bit as strange as the smell that now seemed to envelop him. She couldn't describe it, but his eyes were not just dark but cold and lifeless, while his skin and hair felt hard and coarse, making what was left of him appear alien, as if this were someone else and not her father. But she had no doubt that it was indeed her beloved Daddy.

"I need to explain something," her mother interjected while reaching over and putting a hand on Iowa's shoulder. "Daddy can't understand. He can hear you, but he can no longer understand words." She hesitated. "You need to move back and take your hand away from him."

Iowa didn't respond. It was clear that she heard her mother – she cringed slightly at the sound of her mother's words – but she refused to follow her instructions. If this was the last time she was to see her Daddy, then nothing but death itself was going to force her to stop touching the man.

"Iowa, dear, you don't understand. You need to stop touching him." She hesitated; she understood her daughter's need to make the final connection with her father, and so she waited a few more seconds until there was no time left. "Now," she shouted.

Iowa jumped up and turned to her mother. She was about to demand a reason for this strange behavior when her mother suddenly pointed to the girl's father. When Iowa turned to look, she noticed something happening to the man. His already-narrow face began to get narrower, his eyes began to shrink back into his skull and become two small circles, and his nose started to arch downward. She also noticed that his body, or what she thought was his body, started contracting and pulling together into a small ball, which seemed smaller that he was capable of being even now, when he had been shrunken by death. But something else happened, something that sent Iowa to the other side of the room, where she stood holding onto her mother and trying unsuccessfully not to look. Her mother didn't flinch, as the man's skin turned a yellowish-white and within seconds appeared to be covered with feathers.

"My God," Iowa shrieked, "he looks like a bird. What's happening to him?"

Iowa's mother grasped Iowa by the shoulders and turned her around to face her. "I wanted to tell you, I wanted to tell you years ago, but he wouldn't let me. At first, he was afraid you would be shocked, but when you got older…we had kept it a secret so long that there didn't seem to be any point in saying anything. I guess we also feared that you would hate him for all the times he was missing."

"I don't understand."

"He was too involved. He was too obsessed to stop for a while. Please, keep your eyes on me. He should have stopped, but by the time that I might have been able to reason with him, it was too late. His mind was changing, and he couldn't stop the changing of his body. Do you understand me? Look at me. It wasn't that he didn't love you or didn't want to stay home. It was simply that he couldn't help himself. His body would change whether he liked it or not, and whenever his body changed, something in his mind would change, too. Look at me! You didn't notice it, because whenever he was human there were still sparks of life left in him – he could still remember you and the feeling was strong enough to keep some of the animal instincts at bay. But it couldn't last forever. The animal eventually took over, and when that happened he began to age very quickly and…and now he's dying. Maybe there could have been more time, but…"

Iowa could hardly believe her ears. Certainly, the woman sounded at times like she was babbling, but Iowa seemed to grasp the concept, which made even less sense. She turned toward her father, but he was gone. In his place was a swan-like bird clearly breathing his last. The animal's breathing was hard and forced, and its beak was partly open. Suddenly, it was over and the animal was dead.

Chapter Two - Somehow Iowa's mother managed . . .

Somehow Iowa's mother managed to secure a proper service for the girl's father, even though no one other than Iowa, her mother, and a couple of out-of-town relatives attended the service at the funeral home. He had been cremated, and the marble urn containing his ashes stood in the center of a long, wooden altar and was flanked on either side by clear vases holding long-stemmed white flowers. Iowa had never seen such beautiful flowers, not even around the lake, and she was positive that she would never forget the kind words the creepy funeral director had offered for the occasion.

"He was a unique person, and we shall treasure his memory forever," the heavy-set, silver-haired director quietly intoned, as he stood behind the long altar and looked, first, at the urn and then at the scanty crowd sitting tearfully in front of him. Patting the top of the urn three or four times as if he, too, was a friend of the deceased, he smiled, nodded his head, and repeated his previous assertion that Iowa's father would not be forgotten.

Iowa stared at the urn. It was, of course, the repository of her father's last remains (and, against her will, she wondered if there were any remnants of feathers among the ashes), but it was also one of the whitest objects she had ever seen, and it contrasted vividly with the director's dull black suit directly behind it. For some reason, the urn made her think of heaven, clouds, white birds, and her father, while the suit conjured up ideas such as death, unhappiness, crude boys, and stupid adults. Iowa didn't like thinking about the bad things in the world, and so she focused her attention on the urn, marveling at the way it reflected the beauty of pure white birds and her father's soul, which were now inextricably linked. The manner in which her father died was still a mystery to her, but she was pleased by its connection to a white bird, which was in all likelihood a swan. But even before that, as long ago as she could remember, Iowa was fascinated by white animals, especially swans and doves, and the fact that her father had become such a beautiful bird now invested them with a marvelous, maybe even magical, quality. These were the most beautiful things in the world, and there was something else inherent in them – maybe it was their gentleness or the stately, almost regal manner in which they moved and interacted with the world around them – that not only complemented the purity of their color, but also made Iowa wish that she could become a swan, just like her father, and swim across the lake while arching and curling her long, graceful neck. Glancing at the director, Iowa noticed that his lips were moving, his hand was still patting her father's urn, and yet he wasn't making a sound – the room was deathly silent. If she had her father's power, she would have changed into a swan and never again associated with most human beings.

Iowa did love her mother, most of the time. But unlike her father, the woman was irrationally stern and always forcing her to do something. If it wasn't homework and chores, then it was being nice to the ugly, old relatives sitting two rows behind her at the service. Her mother sometimes allowed her to see friends on weekends, but more often than not Iowa was forced to sneak out of the house (slipping out the back door by the kitchen and jumping over the fence) to visit them at the lake. Luckily, over the last few months her mother had been too preoccupied with Daddy's health to notice when Iowa was gone – on the few times when she had noticed, however, she grounded Iowa or levied some other equally unjust sentence. 'Yes, if only I had my father's power,' she mused, 'I would leave and never come back. I would live somewhere far away from the meanness and cruelty of mother and all the rest of them, parents, teachers, and even some of the students.' When the director had finally finished his eulogy, he excused himself so that the family could have some time to themselves to grieve or chat quietly about the "dearly departed." It was then that Iowa suddenly felt alone and at the mercy of her mother and the relatives who would unceasingly pester her with their apologies and expressions of sympathy.

It was inconceivable that the only relatives that Iowa had were on her mother's side. For years, Iowa had been told that her father's only remaining family – a brother, whom neither she nor her mother had ever met – had died years ago of some mysterious illness, the same illness that had claimed his parents and apparently her own father. Whether this meant that they had all become birds, Iowa was at a loss to say and didn't relish asking her mother for more information either now or at some other more opportune time. The truly unfortunate thing in Iowa's eyes was that her mother's sole relatives consisted of Mr. and Mrs. Smith, individuals whom she vaguely knew and completely abhorred.

The Smiths were large people, much bigger than Iowa's mother, and they always seemed out of breath, as if merely moving taxed their physical capabilities. Mr. Smith had an odd black mustache that seemed longer on one side than the other, while Mrs. Smith was wearing a low-cut black dress that would have looked better on a woman half her age and weight. In fact, while she didn't know the ages of the respective Smiths, they looked much older than either her mother or her father (except maybe on his deathbed), more like someone's grandparents than an aunt and uncle. Iowa was not in the least surprised to hear that the couple was childless, which her mother once attributed to Mrs. Smith's osteoporosis, and a shudder ran through her body when Mrs. Smith announced, after the conclusion of the service, that she loved Iowa like a daughter and that she and Iowa would become very close now that Iowa's father had gone to a better place. Only seconds after the director left, Mrs. Smith sat down in the empty chair next to Iowa and, resting a plump arm across the top of Iowa's chair, asked the girl how she felt after her father's death. "You were at his bedside, I believe, weren't you? Mr. Smith and I were always fond of your father, although I must say that his idea was…incongruous."

Iowa sat upright and turned her whole body toward the woman. "I don't know what you mean," she said defiantly, glowering at Mrs. Smith, whose gray hair was tightly wound behind her head.

Mrs. Smith smiled graciously, as if she had expected such a reaction. "I was only saying that I was sorry he didn't pay more attention to his family. He was…"

"My Daddy loved me, and I don't care whether you knew it or not. I don't know how you can come here and say something bad about him."

"Please don't get upset, dearie," Mrs. Smith smiled. "I'm afraid I misspoke. You are absolutely correct – he did love you, very much, I am told. I am sorry he is gone."

"No, you're not." Iowa got up and stormed over to a different section of the chapel, where she avoided looking at the Smiths and waited for her mother to take her home.

Later, on the ride home, Iowa's mother scolded her for being unkind to Mrs. Smith and ignoring Mr. Smith.

"You were rude. Mrs. Smith was upset by the way you spoke to her. She couldn't believe that I was raising a child to behave in such a manner. I suppose it's a good thing that you didn't say a word to Mr. Smith, even when he expressed his condolences. I don't know what's gotten into you lately, but whatever it is, it has to stop now. Right now, do you hear me?"

"Why are you mad at me? Did she tell you what she said about Daddy?" It was just like her mother, Iowa thought, always taking someone's side over hers.

"You need to be nice to them…"

"Why do I have to be nice to them? What's so special about them? They give me the creeps, and it's lucky they didn't have any children."

"You stop that right now," her mother practically shouted. The car swerved as she turned to look at her daughter.

Neither Iowa nor her mother said another word until they pulled into the driveway of their small, one-story bungalow. The house was like every other house in the neighborhood, except for its peeling paint, lime-green shutters (shutters were either black or white), and unkempt yard (Iowa's mother had trouble pushing the old lawnmower through the thick grass, while Iowa did her best to avoid the hard, time-intensive labor of caring for the lawn). Even though this was the only house that she had ever known, Iowa felt nothing for the place except for the fact that it was much closer to the park than the houses of her friends. Indeed, it was the last of a line of bungalows that ended at the very edge of the park, and Iowa could run from the house to the lake in nearly half the time it took the others just to reach the park. From the kitchen window, Iowa had a perfect view of the grassy open space at the beginning of the park, after which the trees rose up and created a nearly black wall of vegetation (when they were in bloom, of course), and nothing was easier at night than to slip out the back door, take ten large steps to the chain-link fence that encircled the house, and, hopping over the fence with a single movement, land on a grassy path that took her to the woods and, once there, meandered through the trees until it ended at a small clearing at the edge of the lake.

Iowa loved the path. She loved how it ran between small trees and around large trees, up small rises and down shallow gullies, and around and sometimes over outcroppings of brownish rock. She loved it especially where it ended, when practically out of nowhere it opened up to a long, grayish lake that was the home to geese, ducks, and, along its edges, the occasional red fox. The park and especially the lake were the only places in the world that truly felt like home to her, and it didn't matter if she was surrounded by her close friends or completely by herself. Sitting at the kitchen table and watching her mother drone on about the Smiths, Iowa longed to escape to the park, and she could imagine herself dashing along the path (at one point stumbling and nearly falling on her face – she recovered in the nick of time by grabbing a convenient branch) until it reached the clearing at the edge of the lake. She could see the logs, rocks, and tufts of grass and mounds of dirt that served as chairs on which she and her friends would sit and watch the geese paddling from one side of the lake to the other, or imagine what it would be like floating on the lake and allowing the current to take them from one place to another.

"You need to listen to me this time, young lady," Iowa's mother was saying for perhaps the tenth time, as they sat facing each other at the kitchen table. Unable to bear the eleventh, Iowa got up and marched into her bedroom, where she fell face down onto her bed. Undeterred, her mother followed her and sat down next to her at the foot of the bed.

"I know this is hard for you," her mother continued, having changed her tone when she entered Iowa's room. "It's hard for me, too, but you have to understand some things before it's too late. If something ever happens to me – and I'm not saying that something will happen to me, but if something does – the Smiths are the only people that can take care of you. It's not an ideal situation, but it's the only one we have unless you want to end up in foster care."

"I'd rather do that," Iowa mumbled into her pillow.

"No, you wouldn't," her mother continued softly. "The Smiths at least have some money, and they're willing to help you with college and whatever else. Look, they're not bad people. They are kind and patient, but their patience isn't unlimited…" The woman hesitated, not wanting to increase Iowa's resistance to them. "Please, Iowa, whether you believe me or not, I am only thinking of your best interests. I'm sorry that we didn't have other family, but that's the way it is and nothing can be done about it now."

"They give me the creeps."

"Trust me, their hearts are in the right place. There's a good chance you'll never have to worry about it, but, like I said, if something ever happens to me…"

Iowa turned around and sat up, facing her mother. For once, she was shocked by the possibility of losing her mother, and despite everything else she really did love the woman. "Please...," she began, but tears flowed into her eyes and she grasped her mother and buried her face into her shoulder. Iowa cried for some time; her mother cried, too. But Iowa herself couldn't tell whether her tears were for her mother or her father, whose presence in the house could be seen everywhere from knick knacks on bookshelves and counters (he kept a small, plaster eagle in the kitchen, on a counter next to the stove) to his clothes and everything else still in his bedroom. Iowa promised herself that, if possible, she would never forget her father, and that she would never live with the Smiths or anyone else if her mother...if her mother was no longer there.

Chapter Three - Iowa was named after the Midwestern state.

Iowa was named after the Midwestern state. That was all her mother ever said, but it didn't matter because she liked the unusual name, and she liked how it set her apart from the other kids with common, pedestrian names. Iowa attended Thornton Middle School, which was about a twenty minute walk in the morning from her house, unless she was late and had to run (the quickest that she had ever made it to school on her own was eight minutes). She was slightly taller than most of the girls in her class, and she had long, blonde hair, a clear face (thankfully), and straight features. She was told that she was attractive – and, indeed, she was slim but not too skinny – but she didn't need to hear that from anyone, particularly her friends, because she could see it in the eyes of the boys who tried to talk to her (except, of course, when she was forced to wear her glasses). However, Iowa wasn't interested in boys, at least not in the way that some of the girls were. She liked some of the boys, but most of them were crude and lacked a feeling for beautiful things such as swans and geese. Iowa appreciated a couple of her teachers, though, particularly Ms. Royce, her science teacher. She was Iowa's favorite.

Ms. Royce was in her late thirties and still quite attractive (according to Iowa and her friends), although she didn't have a significant other at the moment and probably hadn't had one in years. Since Ms. Royce's class was the last of the day, Iowa and her friends often stayed after class to chat to her and to ask her advice on any number of issues. Over the two years that they had known Ms. Royce, they had learned that the love of her life had died in a boating accident a number of years ago and that she had a cat named Cat, two goldfish named Fish (One and Two), and a fondness for all kinds of deer, which she thought were some of the most amazing creatures found in the woods near the school. Ms. Royce was pleasant and sympathetic, like Iowa's father, and because she too had experienced the death of someone very close, she was able to commiserate with Iowa over her loss, which she had noticed in the obituaries of the local paper. Except for Ms. Royce, Iowa didn't want anyone else to know about her father's death. She didn't want to explain the circumstances of her father's death (if indeed it was possible to explain the circumstances), and she didn't want to hear the hollow expressions of sympathy, which, as far as she was concerned, were nothing more than manifestations of happiness that the loss was hers and not theirs. It was different with Ms. Royce, and Iowa was glad that she had found out.

"I think I understand, but I won't pretend that I have felt exactly what you feel or that my experience was exactly the same as yours. In any case, death is never easy, especially if it takes you by surprise and threatens to change your feelings or perceptions about the deceased," Ms. Royce had told her after school that day.

She was sitting on the corner of her desk, while Iowa was in her usual seat, in the front row just to the left of Ms. Royce's desk. Ms. Royce smiled wanly, and Iowa noticed that in her eyes was the same kindness that she had seen in her father's eyes, at least before the end came. "It's not easy to lose a parent, particularly when you're young, and I suspect that it shattered the security and continuity that you expected to last a lifetime. I can only imagine how vulnerable you must feel as a result. I think you once told me that besides your mother, you had no other relatives. Is that right? I remember when Charles died. Again, I am not comparing my loss with yours, but at the time it seemed like the world had come to an end. Perhaps for a few moments it did, because I tried to run away from the fact and everything else that might have helped me cope – that might have brought me back to humanity where, in the end, we all belong. I suppose for me things changed when I realized that I still had the best of him with me, that I would always have that part of him, guiding me and helping me to understand how to live – and how not to live. It's a curious thing, but I still feel close to him when I'm happy, and sometimes I can't help smiling when I make a decision that I know that he would never have made. It's hard to explain, except that I am more in control of my life than I ever was when he was living – and that's a good thing." Iowa felt better after having listened to Ms. Royce, and she felt without quite knowing why that Ms. Royce understood what she was facing in the absence of her father, with the mortality of her mother, and the existence of the Smiths.

During lunch the following day, Iowa and the other the Cygnets chatted about a lot of things – girls, boys, creepy Jimmy, teachers, the lake, parents – including the death of her father. The Cygnets – four girls (including Iowa) and one boy who were in the same grade and had been fast friends since kindergarten, if not before – were the only other people with whom Iowa could talk about her father's death, her mother, the Smiths, and everything else that had a personal impact on her life. She didn't disclose the intimate details of her father's last hours, but she told them virtually everything else, including the possibility of ending up with the "repulsive" Smiths if something were to happen to her mother.

"You can stay with me," Press, the oldest Cygnet (by six months), interjected. "I'm sure my parents wouldn't mind. If they did, you could hide in my room or in the apartment over the garage, where my grandmother lived before she died." Press was serious, and neither she nor the others could see any problems with such a plan. But just to be certain, the others – Lu, Dana, and Luke, the only boy in the group – echoed her willingness to help and shelter Iowa, if she needed it. And each of them in their own way had expressed their horror of the Smiths (although none of them actually knew the Smiths) and their condolences to Iowa, for both the loss of her father and the potential catastrophe that awaited her should her mother pass away.

The Cygnets were like family to Iowa. In fact, all five of them had declared that they had no family but themselves – or, at least, that the Cygnets were the most important members of their families – and that they would stick together through thick and thin, allowing no one either to disrupt their relationship or to become part of the Cygnets. A number of years ago, Jimmy, another boy in the same class, a boy who was often mean spirited, derisively called the group the four and a half Musketeers (the half referring to Luke), a name that stuck to the group for about a half year. (Others, too, felt left out, because Iowa, Press, Lu, Dana, and Luke didn't care to associate with anyone else when they were all together.) After the name faded, Iowa noted one day out of the blue that it would be fun to have a name permanently to remind themselves of the closeness of their relationship – although she didn't like Jimmy's appellation (or Jimmy himself) – and she suggested the Cygnets. Although she didn't tell the others that her father once called her a cygnet after she had put on a lovely, white princess dress for Halloween, she did say that the name was fitting because they all thought swans were beautiful and because cygnets were found at lakes like the one in the park. Surprisingly, the others immediately agreed, and from then on the others called themselves the Five Cygnets or, more simply, the Cygnets.

There were no rivalries or jealousies among the Cygnets, because no single individual was more favored or better liked than another. They were truly Musketeers (though not in the way that Jimmy meant), and they truly believed what they said about one another, that they were family and that no one would ever separate them. Iowa, for her part, couldn't have said which Cygnets she

liked best or which was first among equals. They were all
wonderful and quirky in their own way, and she wouldn't have
chosen one over the other for any reason. Press, the tallest of the
group, taller even than Iowa, was thin and athletic. She spoke in a
loud, rapid patter, as if running a race, although sometimes she
could be calm and deliberative, if the occasion demanded, unless
someone other than the Cygnets criticized one of her favorite
sports teams or, especially, the Cygnets themselves. When that
happened, Press could be quite vocal, furiously so. Dana, on the
other hand, was the most intellectual of the group (she had read
extensively on Cygnets after the group decided on the name), and
she naturally tended to be cautious and deliberative when she was
speaking, although when the mood was just right she could match
Press patter for patter. The other students, though, never saw that
side of her, and they considered her reserved and retiring, maybe
even shy, because she was slightly overweight and had a silver
dollar-size birthmark on her right temple. On the contrary, Press
didn't look on these attributes as disadvantages – she didn't care
what the others thought and generally wouldn't have associated
with the other kids at school, regardless of her weight and
birthmark. Lu was fairly nondescript -- average in height, average
in grades, average in outlook – and although she had no trouble
interacting with other people, she rarely looked anyone in the face
when she spoke to them, preferring instead to stare at some
invisible object near her feet. She may have been shy, but the
Cygnets couldn't tell because she acted the same way with

everyone. Overall, she was genuinely kind and absolutely loyal to the Cygnets. And Luke…well, Luke was Luke. The only boy that the other Cygnets thought it fit to associate with, he was quiet and reserved with others, and he was really only himself with Dana, Press, Lu, and of course Iowa. He was studious, he had little interest in sports or the games that the other boys played, and he often puzzled over how he could make a living when he was older selling stamps. He loved collecting stamps, especially stamps with lots of bright colors, and, more than anything else except the Cygnets, he loved dogs, especially golden retrievers, especially his own dog Butch. Jimmy, in front of a group of classmates, once asked Luke what he would like to be if he could be anything. Jimmy had in mind a profession, but when Luke responded, "a golden retriever," Jimmy thought it was so funny (and stupid) that he told everyone that Luke wanted to be a dog so "he could poop on everyone's lawn."

The Cygnets, who couldn't believe their luck in living in the same neighborhood, attending the same school, and being of a single mindset regarding the other Cygnets, met each school day at lunch, where they would find a table or space to themselves to discuss the latest news of interest to themselves, such as the death of Iowa's father and the creepy way that Jimmy had of hovering just outside their gatherings. He didn't try to intrude, although he was often obnoxious when speaking about the way they stuck together (and, he doubtless thought, excluded him). The Cygnets ignored him; they refused to waste their time and energy on him when they could be making plans for the weekend, which usually entailed a walk through the park to a small clearing at the edge of the lake.

The weekends were special to the Cygnets. The weekends were truly the only times when they could gather without students, teachers, or other busybodies milling about. The weekends were the only times when the Cygnets could truly be a family, going about their business without parents, siblings, or others intruding, and without the demands of homework, chores, or even funerals. Sometimes, the Cygnets met at one of their houses, where, if they were lucky, they would congregate by themselves in a basement, garage, or bedroom and go about their business; sometimes, if the weather was suitable and the neighbors were out of sight, they might gather in the corner of a backyard and pretend that no one but themselves existed. However, if they had a choice, they always preferred the lake, which was no more than a thirty minute walk from the house farthest from the water's edge, which, to be exact, was Lu's house (she lived two streets behind Iowa and a couple of blocks father up from the park).

The lake – as well as the park itself -- was generally free from the neighborhood families, even near the water, probably because there were really no broad areas, no fresh lawns to lounge in on a warm summer afternoon, or any place to launch a small boat on the lake, which was too shallow anyway for all but rowboats. To get to the lake, one had to cross a couple of broad, open fields of dirt and weeds that gradually merged into small hills covered with more weeds and then, a little farther on, more hills and tall, lush trees. The Cygnets (probably Lu, although none of them remembered for sure) had long ago discovered a path that led from the first tree one encountered, along a small stream that meandered toward the lake, and finally to the lake itself, where it ended in the small, oval clearing in which logs, rounded rocks, and clumps of dirt had been manipulated to form chairs on which the Cygnets would lounge and chat away the day without parents, siblings, classmates, and others who might divert their attention toward things of little importance. There was even an old swing (little more than an old rope with several large knots in it) that dangled from a large, drooping branch of an old tree that reached out far enough over the water that one could swing out from the shore and land in water that was waist high. No one knew where the rope had come from (it had been dangling over the water long before the first Cygnet had crept close enough to the lake's edge to stick a big toe into the lake's warm water), but it provided hours of pleasure, especially on warm summer evenings when the stars were bright, pinpoint lights that quickly blurred and disappeared as the water washed over one's face and head.

On any given evening together, the Cygnets might spend a fair amount of time chatting (usually about school, classmates, teachers, siblings, neighbors, and sometimes girls and boys), playing cards or board games that accommodated five players, or simply bouncing around for no particular reason. If they were at the lake, however, they might play hide and seek (it never got old no matter how old they got), conduct park explorations of one kind or another, or augment the clearing or some other area in the park with items either found in the park (sticks, rocks, bushes) or brought from home (broken toys, abandoned chairs, discarded broom handles) that would provide a homey touch and allow them, at other times, to lounge near the water's edge and soak up the sun, the stars, or both. Sometimes, they would play Sticks. Sticks combined elements of sword fighting (the swords were often elaborate creations made from tree branches, twigs, and other items) and hide and seek. Unlike most of the other games, though, Sticks had no consistent rules – that is to say, there were indeed rules, often detailed prescriptions of what one could and couldn't do during the game, but the rules changed every time they played the game and, in fact, a significant part of the game was spent devising the rules, which the Cygnets carefully followed to prevent penalties or the forfeiture of the game. In a recent game, for example, the Cygnets identified a starting and ending point for the game (a large rock half way in and out of the water) and then paired up, flipping a quarter to determine who was on which team (the odd Cygnet being both judge and member of whatever team won). One team (determined by another flip of the coin) ran into the trees to hide, while the other team closed their eyes and proceeded to count to one hundred. When the number was reached, more or less, the counters set off to find the hiders and, when found (without too much trouble), a sword fight ensued to determine which team could return to the starting point and claim victory. Not surprisingly, victory wasn't quite that simple, since there was no clear resolution to the sword fight and since Press and Iowa (players on opposing teams) both reached the rock at the same time, according to the judge who arrived at the same time as the other players. Despite the ambiguity of the ending, everyone was happy and ready for another round of sticks, albeit under slightly different rules.

Iowa was at the lake with the other Cygnets when she decided to talk about the death of her father. She wouldn't have spoken to anyone else about her farther, nor would she have spoken about him at any other place, even though she still didn't divulge all the details. "I can't say that I knew him well," she began to say, dangling her right big toe into the lake's water while the others sat on logs or the ground a couple of feet away. The sun had just dipped below the horizon, and Cygnets were resting from a vigorous game of Sticks that started with a semblance of rules but ended in a free-for-all in which rules seemed to be made up on the spot. "I think I loved him and all that, and he was without doubt the nicest person in the world, but he was sick all the time and refused to come out of his room. He probably didn't want anyone else to get whatever he had. It was hard to deal with rarely seeing him; if I had more time with him, I could have told him that I loved him." She hesitated, stifled a cry, and sat quietly for a couple of minutes before continuing. No one interrupted her. "He showed me some amazing things, though, and maybe someday I'll share them with you."

"Like what?" Lu inquired, piqued by her friend's secrecy, which was rare among friends such as these.

"I can't tell you now. You're going to have to trust me on this. Some day when the time is just right…"

"What's the big secret," Luke chimed in.

"No, really it's nothing, except that I loved him and I…well, I loved him, that's all. I don't want to talk about it anymore, because it is going to make me cry."

Lu caught sight of a small fox running along the edge of the trees before disappearing into the increasingly dark woods. The sudden appearance of the fox gave Iowa and everyone else a chance to change the subject.

That evening, Iowa wondered if she should have told them more about her father. She had no doubt that they would believe her, but she wondered if they would assume that she too could change into an animal when she was sick. It was a natural thing to ask, and so she decided to keep quiet about this until there was a better time, if ever.

Chapter Four - The friends stayed true to one another

The days, weeks, and months passed since the death of her father, and the friends stayed true to one another, as close to each other as they had always been. School continued as it always had and always would, the members of the Cygnets had their various ups and downs – Luke, for example, was forced to spend the summer in Europe with his family, meaning that his connections with the Cygnets were mainly through postcards and other obsolete media and Iowa's father had become a topic of little interest to Iowa and the other members.

The Cygnets continued to meet in Luke's absence, and when he finally returned they all had a private celebration at the lake, where it was still warm enough to swim and play in the water. But something had happened during that time. No one really noticed the change except Iowa, because it affected her more than the others. When Luke looked at her, he didn't look at her like he looked at the others; he stared at her, letting his eyes circle her face and then run up and down her body, smiling as he did so. Several times, Iowa caught Luke looking at her while her back was turned (she would turn quickly, innocently, and catch him in the act). Neither she nor Luke said anything – after all, she wasn't completely certain that anything had changed despite his stares, and he was still a member in good standing with the Cygnets, and there was nothing in the world that she would do to change that or the peace and harmony of the group. He was still shy, but she couldn't help feeling that at least part of his reticence now resulted from something else. But, again, no one else seemed to notice anything unusual, and Luke did nothing more than look and smile when he seemed certain that no one but she was watching.

Shortly after Luke's return another event shook the Cygnets, especially Iowa. Just before the start of the new school year, she was sent to stay with the Smiths for two weeks. She had adamantly opposed visiting them, especially without her mother, but she didn't have any choice in the matter and, furthermore, her mother insisted – no, demanded – that she get to know them and appreciate their kindness. Maybe it was her resistance, or the strange ways the Smiths had (they never stayed up late, although they didn't care if Iowa did, and they didn't own a TV, and so they spent their short evenings reading books and newspapers. Furthermore, they weren't talkers: They spoke from time to time, generally exchanging pleasantries or book recommendations, and they were disgustingly curious about Iowa's school and plans for the future, which, they emphasized, she needed to consider now, not later, not after it's too late), or the fact that their house had a peculiar smell to it – not the kind of smell that had permeated her father's room, but something different, something aggressively human, as if they had removed all traces of anything resembling animals and what was left was the Smiths, or human beings in a world without animal life. She didn't know how to describe it, but whatever it was it added to the overall unpleasantness of being away from home and the Cygnets, and it put her in a bad mood that lasted for at least a month after she returned.

Naturally, Iowa was mad at the Smiths – they never left her alone, they always wanted to talk about something personal to her (her friends, her desires, her life at home, her interest in animals), and they kept prying into her reactions to her father's death, which they would broach by asking her about her understanding of death. "Let's talk about your father's death," Mrs. Smith began one night over the dinner table, her fingers and lips shiny from the fried chicken she was eating. "I am told that there was something unusual about it. Perhaps this was due to his suffering, but whatever it might have been, it is a healthy response to speak about troubling things, don't you agree, dear?" She looked at Iowa and then Mr. Smith, and then back to Iowa.

Iowa didn't take the bait, and cut the inquiry short by denying that she was with her father when he died. "Mother wouldn't allow me in the room," she added with a slight, condescending smile. But if Iowa was mad at the Smiths, she was even madder at her mother for subjecting her to such indignities, and she was even mildly upset with the Cygnets, because they didn't contact her when she was gone and, afterwards, failed to understand the depths of her suffering over that period of time.

Of course, Iowa was over everything – at least with respect to the Cygnets – by the end of the first quarter, when Luke informed the Cygnets one Saturday at the lake that his dog, Butch, had died the night before. Later that same week, Press, with the other Cygnets sitting around a relatively quiet table at lunch, asked if she could invite one of the boys from the lacrosse team to join the Cygnets. "He's really nice," she added, as if that made a difference. While she accepted the group's near unanimous decision (Press was the outlier), she occasionally missed a Friday or Saturday gathering of the Cygnets to see the young man in question.

Something peculiar also happened that quarter. One sunny afternoon as the Cygnets were either swimming or splashing in the lake, Iowa was about to wade into the water when she noticed a small net floating about six inches from the shore. The net was only a few inches from end to end, and at first glance it appeared to be just another piece of debris bobbing up and down on the water's surface. But as she looked at it, observing the way that the water rippled and swirled around it, she couldn't help taking a closer look. Getting down on her hands and knees and peering into the net, Iowa spotted a small fish or fish-like creature (it looked sort of like a fish, but its oddly-shaped fins and sparkling scales made her wonder if it was something else) and, as she moved closer, practically putting her face into the water, it became clear that the creature was tangled up in the net's threads and struggling to free itself. Iowa decided not to call the others to have a look (they were too busy to look at one small fish among thousands in the lake), and so she watched the creature as it twisted and turned and wrapped itself tighter and tighter in the net. After a while, the creature had become so tightly enmeshed in the threads that it could no longer move, or else it had realized the futility of its efforts and had given up and waited for death to rescue it.

A profound sadness suddenly swept over Iowa, and for a few minutes it took nearly all her self-restraint to keep from crying. What troubled her, however, was not the creature's plight (although that was certainly unpleasant to watch), but something else, something undefinable, something that she knew was important but that for some reason was unable to grasp. "I want to feel sorry for you," she whispered to the creature, "but something is telling me I shouldn't be or I can't. It doesn't make sense. If it's true, then what should I be sorry for? Myself? I can't cry for myself." Unable to make sense of her feelings, Iowa reached down into the warm water and began to free the small creature from the netting. Within seconds, the netting began to loosen and the creature appeared to be nearly free, but then something happened – Iowa turned the net the wrong way or a loop that she thought would unravel the net actually tightened it – and the netting started to get tighter and tighter until her efforts only succeed in killing the poor creature. Looking at the limp thing in the palm of her hand, the netting fused to its body as if it were part of the creature itself, Iowa knew that she had done something terribly wrong -- or that she was going to do something wrong – and in a fury to relieve herself of the emotional burden, she threw the creature and netting far off into the woods. Iowa waded over to the others, and no sooner had seen their laughing faces than she forgot about the creature and was splashing, screaming, and laughing as wildly as everyone else.

One week later, Iowa's mother died.

Chapter Five - Three days prior to this event

Three days prior to this event, Iowa's mother suddenly collapsed on the kitchen floor and had to be helped to her room. It was a cool Wednesday evening when it happened, and Iowa and her mother had just finished dinner and were washing the dishes. Initially, both were convinced that the woman was suffering from mild indigestion, but as the night wore on and the pain began to spread throughout her body, Iowa's mother realized that it was more serious, although she didn't inform her daughter right away. She didn't want to scare her, and she also wanted to make arrangements before Iowa had a chance to worry.

The following day, Iowa was surprised by the sudden appearance of the Smiths. But when her mother called Iowa into her bedroom, the girl realized that everything she knew and understood had suddenly changed.

Iowa's mother was in bed, on her back, and covered with a heavy blanket that reached up and around her neck. Her head was propped up by several, thick pillows. The woman didn't look sick, not exactly, although she appeared old and frail, as if she had aged twenty years since yesterday's dinner.

She was silent as Iowa entered the room, and when the girl carefully closed the door behind her and turned to her mother, the woman could tell right away that she understood what was happening. Her mother could see it on the girl's face. 'There is beauty and wisdom in my child,' the woman told herself when she saw the knowing expression on her daughter's face and observed the girl's moist, sympathetic eyes, which were locked on her own. She congratulated herself on having such a wonderful daughter, but no sooner had a faint smile creased her lips than it quickly fell, pulling down the rest of her facial features with it. Something horrible had passed through her consciousness. Looking at her daughter, the woman realized that time was short and felt certain that her wonderful daughter would disappear as soon as she closed her eyes. It wasn't right, she told herself, to leave this earth while Iowa was still a child; and it wasn't right to be deprived of the blessings every parent has a right to expect from the first moment she holds her baby in her arms. She wasn't going to see Iowa grow and mature, and she wasn't going to share the girl's joy when meeting the right man, when marrying the man and having children, children every bit as wonderful as Iowa herself. She wasn't going to experience any of this, and the unexpected realization of her misfortune weighed heavily on the old woman, as if a giant beast had perched itself on her chest. Iowa's mother would have howled to the heavens, but the beast was too large and too heavy for her to push it aside to release her sorrows.

For a few minutes, mother and daughter were silent and, while her mother breathed heavily (a faint gurgling noise emanated from the back of her throat), Iowa reached under the covers and grasped the old woman's cold, bony hand.

However, this was not the time to remain silent. Iowa's mother knew that she had to muster the strength to remove the beast if she had any chance of telling her daughter everything she needed to know before it was too late. Once, twice, the old woman tried to say something to her daughter, but she could only muster a few deep, halting breaths and some disconnected noises that resembled words but contained no sense, at least not to Iowa's ears. With Iowa now leaning closer to her mother, the woman took several deep breaths and momentarily closed her eyes and, squeezing Iowa's hand, she forced the beast aside and regained the strength necessary to speak to her daughter.

Iowa's mother first apologized for bringing the Smiths, but emphasized that they would not take her away before the end of the school year. Until then, they would stay with her at the house, and life would go on as it always did, albeit without her. She paused to gather her strength. But there was more. There was something that she needed to explain before it was too late. Ever since Iowa's father had died, her mother had debated within herself whether or not to tell the girl more, to explain her father's incredible change, which she herself was able to perform but refused to do for Iowa's sake. But she was now at a point in which a decision had to be made, and there were so many reasons on either side that she decided that the truth was best, especially since she couldn't be certain that her end wouldn't be similar to her husband's.

"You need to understand," the sick woman was saying, "You can't play with this. People don't understand. Your father didn't understand, and…" She began coughing, and then settled down and a little bit of color came back into her face. "You only have one choice, and after that you can never choose again, you can never revoke that choice. It will always be you. But, at least in the beginning, you have the power over the change. You can change at will, although it should only be for short intervals. That was your father's mistake. And then," she continued, not entirely coherently, "if you make a mistake, if you stay too long, you will begin to think and act like an animal and…and the power of changing may be taken from you." The gurgling in the back of her throat became noticeable and she began to breath erratically, after which she closed her eyes and fell asleep.

Iowa wasn't entirely certain what her mother was trying to explain, but she was positive that it had to do with her father's transformation into a bird and what had happened to him because he wasn't careful. Beyond this, however, she didn't know why her mother wanted to speak about Daddy, since it happened a long time ago and there were probably other things of greater importance that needed to be discussed. Iowa didn't have the heart to wake her mother; she would have slipped out of the room to give the woman time to rest, but the Smiths were in the other room, and the last thing she wanted to do was to associate with those people.

Over the following two days, Iowa's mother slept fitfully and opened her eyes only now and then seeming to impart some important message to her daughter who remained by her mother's bedside practically throughout the entire ordeal. While there were times when the woman was incoherent or began to say something only to fall asleep before finishing her line of thought, she somehow managed to tell Iowa everything that she wanted to say, including the fact the she loved her and regretted leaving this earth before witnessing Iowa's graduation and the birth of her own children. She also regretted leaving her to someone else, which no mother should ever have to do and which she would probably be punished in the afterlife for having done so. "My God," she said just before closing her eyes for the last time. She reached out for her daughter while gasping "Iowa," but couldn't find the girl before her arm fell useless at her side.

Iowa had been saddened by the death of her mother, more so, in fact, than she would have believed only a few months earlier. They had grown much closer when her mother fell ill, and even if the Smiths hadn't been lying in wait for Iowa, she would have gladly stayed with her mother, helping her transition to another life. After the funeral, Iowa, who throughout everything had seemed brave and confident, suddenly broke down and remained in her room the rest of the day and for most of the succeeding day. She did venture out from time to time, but that was only to take care of necessities and, during this and every other time, she refused to exchange more than simple pleasantries with the Smiths. Iowa had reached the point at which she despised the couple, hating them for what they planned to do to her, and yet she did her best not to show her distaste of them, since the last thing she wanted to do was to antagonize them and encourage them to put their moving plans into action. Iowa couldn't help recalling that she had once blamed her mother for the mere existence of the Smiths. But once she had forgiven her mother, she realized that the woman was only doing her duty, thinking about what was best for her daughter when she was no longer around to protect her. Yes, her mother made a poor choice, but it was a choice, and a well-meaning choice, she conceded, was better than nothing. Nevertheless, Iowa wished that her mother had given her more credit for being mature and grownup, and had at least discussed the situation more fully with her before the end. Of course, if her mother had given her the benefit of the doubt, Iowa would have been hard pressed to know how to take care of herself, other than to avoid the Smiths at all costs. Luckily, there was still some time before the end of the school year.

One week after the funeral, while she was sitting down to dinner with the Smiths, Iowa wondered why the deaths of her parents were so different. Dying was dying, and yet her father suffered from the disquieting changes, which didn't affect her mother, and there were other things, things she couldn't quite understand, that were not only troubling but for some reason seemed to involve her. It wasn't clear, and it was slightly troubling in a way that a major test is, if you hadn't studied for it. Iowa was playing with her steak at the time – after having cut it into small pieces, she began to pile the pieces on top of one another to see how great a tower she could construct (to the dismay of Mr. Smith, who didn't approve of playtime at the dinner table. He would have put a stop to the nonsense, but held back because of Iowa's grief and because of Mrs. Smith's expression when she saw what he was about to do) – when it occurred to her that apart from the changes, the only real difference between their deaths was the smell – her father's room smelled like wild animals, while her mother's room smelled like fresh linen. Iowa's steak tower collapsed at this realization, which opened Iowa's eyes even if it didn't completely answer the question of the difference and what it meant for her and possibly the Cygnets. 'Why the Cygnets?' she asked herself. But just as the answer to this question seemed to be creeping into her consciousness, it was immediately lost when Mrs. Smith broke her concentration by speaking to her.

"Iowa, darling," Mrs. Smith said quietly in a sweet voice that was almost musical. Iowa hated it when Mrs. Smith used the term "darling," because it was a term of endearment and Iowa didn't want to be endearing to the Smiths, and to her there was nothing endearing about the Smiths. "Mr. Smith and I are heartily sorry for the passing of your mother. Now, we are going to do everything we can to get things all straightened up – legal-wise, you understand – and so you don't have to worry your little head about a single thing, darling. Everything will be just fine, especially after the end of the year when you come back with us to…"

"To that old house you live in?" Iowa tried to be civil, but the thought of leaving and moving in with the Smiths taxed every ounce of self-control she had.

"Yes, darling. We've already set up a bedroom for you, and we can bring a few of your things there when we move."

"What? Not all of my things?"

"Well, some of it is just…"

"I want all of my things," she replied, suspecting that she had taken Mrs. Smith's bait. "You have all your things, why can't I have all mine?"

"Of course, our house – and it will be yours, too – is, as you know, a little small…" She looked at Iowa and noticed the sullen look on the child's face. "But yes, yes, you're right. We need to do something to accommodate your needs. Let's talk about it another time before we leave. Is that okay, darling?"

Iowa didn't respond. She pushed her plate away, got up from the table, and walked to the front door. As she walked out, she informed the Smiths over her left shoulder that she was going for a walk.

"Darling, don't be late. Remember, you have school tomorrow." Mrs. Smith wasn't sure whether Iowa heard her, but she decided not to press the child, not yet, at least. "Children need space at times like these," she mused pleasantly and, turning to her Mr. Smith, "but, I agree, not indefinitely."

Iowa had intended to go to the lake, since she knew that her friends would be there, but for some reason she changed her mind and walked around the neighborhood, looking casually at the houses and counting the ones that were dark inside. The sun had long since slipped below the horizon, and the street lights were blazing overhead, attracting countless flying bugs that banged headlong over and over against the light globes. Iowa didn't know how long she was gone, but when she finally returned the table was empty and the dishes had all been cleaned. Mr. Smith had gone to his room by that time, and Mrs. Smith, who had been waiting by the front door, welcomed Iowa back and suggested, in passing, that she not be out so late again, especially on a school night.

Chapter Six - Iowa met up with the Cygnets as usual

The following day at school, Iowa met up with the Cygnets as usual, and they all chatted and laughed and made plans for the weekend as if nothing had happened. They asked Iowa where she had been, why she hadn't been to the lake, and why no one had answered her phone. Iowa, reluctant to revisit the death of her mother and the presence of the Smiths, explained that she had visitors and that she was forced to entertain them and didn't have time for anything else, not even a short phone call. She offered her apologies and promised that she would again never go a day without speaking one or more of the Cygnets. However, she added remotely, as if something invisible were floating on the horizon, the visitors were still at her house and would likely be there for some time, to the end of the school year, at least.

Iowa was reluctant to say anything more. In the first place, she didn't want to think about what awaited her at home or, more significantly, at the end of the school year, which was still a few months away. In the second place, she hadn't told the Cygnets about her mother's illness – at the time, she wasn't able to think of anyone or anything else apart from her mother – and now that she could say something, she felt uncomfortable having kept it from them, lying about the Smiths and what had happened at home, and simply couldn't bring herself to admit that she had betrayed their confidences. She planned to tell them everything later on, but right now she lacked the strength to do anything more than to revel in the moment, to absorb the happiness that always infused her relations with the Cygnets. Luckily, they didn't seem to be overly interested in newspapers, and so they would not likely hear about her mother's death for some time, or until she decided to break the news.

Although Iowa looked like her usual self, Press noticed that she wasn't as jokey as she usually was ("jokey" was Press's current favorite word), and so she asked Iowa facetiously if she had just won the lottery.

"What do you mean?" she asked, fearing that Press knew something and was trying to ferret it out of her.

"Nothing. I only meant that…well, you don't seem very happy. Is there something wrong?"

Iowa smiled wanly at Press and then at the others. Just then the bell rang for everyone to go back to class. As they were getting up to leave, Iowa touched Press's arm to get her attention. "Everything is fine. We can talk later."

Later that afternoon, Ms. Royce was handing back essays that the students had written on jobs in science. She had asked the students to research a job or profession in science, note some of the interesting aspects of the job (that is, those aspects that might make the job worth pursuing), and then say something about the educational requirements of the job. Ms. Royce's goal was to help the students consider careers in science, but at the same time she wanted to get the students thinking about how to make their lives meaningful. "Too many people," she had once said, "simply take jobs or train for jobs without really thinking about whether the work can provide long-term satisfaction. Of course, you also have to find out what is satisfying and what you expect out of life, but if you don't start doing it now, you could wake up in a situation that's maybe okay, but you can't change. Can you imagine wanting to be a ballet dancer only to find that out when you're fifty years old – and by then it's too late to take the plunge." While she didn't expect science careers to be for everyone, and she was too experienced to expect any but a handful of students to take the assignment and her words to heart, she was nevertheless pleased with most of the results and, as she handed back the essays, she couldn't help adding a word or two of praise as she did. Ms. Royce, however, hesitated when she came to Iowa. Standing in front of the girl's desk, looking at her with narrow eyes as if something was troubling her, Ms. Royce silently placed Iowa's paper on her desk. "Can you stay a minute after class?" Ms. Royce asked Iowa.

After everyone had gone except Iowa, Ms. Royce came over and sat down in the desk in front of her. Sitting erect and looking into Iowa's eyes, she clicked her tongue absently and then began speaking in a soft, almost reverent voice.

"You're different today. I look at you, and I can see something has changed. In your essay, you wrote about being a veterinarian so you could help animals. But I am beginning to see you're no longer that person. Helping animals is the last thing on your mind now. Am I right?"

Iowa squirmed in her chair. She didn't know what Ms. Royce meant by saying that she no longer wanted to help animals, but it was clear that her teacher had something else in mind and that she wasn't concerned about Iowa's desire to help animals. What Ms. Royce was getting at, though, was not only a mystery but it also made her uncomfortable, as if she had done something wrong.

"Yes," Iowa replied after a prolonged silence. She looked over Ms. Royce's left shoulder and through the window behind her. The sun was bright and unrelenting, and there were few if any clouds in the sky, which meant that the Cygnets would gather at the lake and that there would be a few moments during which she didn't have to remember recent events and could forget this strange discussion. "Yes," she continued, without looking at Ms. Royce. "Yes, there are other things on my mind." For some reason, having admitted to Ms. Royce that today was different than other days, Iowa couldn't hold back and told Ms. Royce what she presumably already knew. "My mother died a few days ago, and I am going to live with the Smiths at the end of the school year. I can't stand the Smiths, and I don't want to leave my friends."

"I'm sorry to hear it, Iowa," Ms. Royce said, and Iowa noticed that she relaxed slightly, as if her confession broke some barrier that had been erected between them. "You're going through a transition that's difficult for anyone. You'll see, things will work out for the best, and there will come a time when your pain will be over and you'll look back on your mother with happiness, not sadness. You may even come to like the Smiths, who, I'm sure, will do everything they can to make your life full and meaningful. Now, if you need someone to talk to, I hope you'll reach out to me."

"I will," Iowa said, not the least interested in speaking to anyone other than the Cygnets.

"Good, I'm glad to hear it." Ms. Royce smiled warmly at Iowa, and then waited for her to say something else, doubtless something she wanted all along, although Iowa was as confused as she was initially with respect to what Ms. Royce truly wanted. This time, though, Iowa's continued silence and her hopeful stare out the window forced Ms. Royce to speak. "I wonder," Ms. Royce said, "if there is something else. Your eyes don't look as bright as they usually do. Maybe it's because of your loss, but, then again, maybe it's something else. Maybe..." Ms. Royce hesitated for a moment or two and, smiling, she stood up, preparing to leave. "Maybe it is your loss," she repeated, "but right now I suspect that it's something else. If you want to tell me, I will certainly listen, but I'm not going to try to force anything out of you. If you don't want to tell me, that's fine; once again, I'm not going to pry. Remember, if you need someone to talk to, please give me a call. We can talk about anything." Ms. Royce smiled again and turned and walked between the desks to the door.

Just before she stepped out of the room, she turned and again looked at Iowa. "You've doubtless learned some wonderful things but be careful. Please, be careful. Once again, I am sorry for your loss." She again smiled warmly, and Iowa could have sworn that Ms. Royce had blinked her left eye.

Iowa watched Ms. Royce leave the room and, as soon as she left the building, observed her through the window walking down the front walk and then disappearing into the faculty parking lot. She was troubled by what Ms. Royce had said. The woman didn't appear to be concerned over the death of Iowa's mother – she treated that as a matter-of-fact event, something that had happened and that because it couldn't be changed, one had to get over it and move on – but instead spoke mysteriously about something else, as if she knew something about Iowa, and yet there was no way that she could have known anything, not even if she had spoken to the Smiths. Something didn't seem right, and yet as Iowa replayed the conversation in her mind as she left the classroom and then the school and school grounds, she eventually decided that there was nothing behind her words. Ms. Royce was simply being Ms. Royce, and Iowa had read too much into what she said, or didn't say, and, besides, Iowa liked Ms. Royce. She liked her more than the other teachers and, in fact, she liked her more than all the other adults that she knew, especially the Smiths. Suddenly, the thought of seeing the Smiths put Iowa in a foul mood and, instead of going home, she went to the lake, hoping that the Cygnets would be there, waiting.

Chapter Seven - The sun's light was still bright

The sun's light was still bright, but by the time she reached the lake, it had turned a rich gold color, giving everything surrounding her – the trees, the bushes, and even the lake itself – a pleasant, mellow hue. The colors were almost dreamlike, and they filled Iowa with a warm, happy feeling.

Iowa was thrilled that the Cygnets were all near the lake when she arrived. They were sitting on logs or tufts of grass in a clearing at the lip of the lake, which for years had been their de facto meeting place. Everyone jumped up when Iowa came into sight, and when she had reached the clearing, they surrounded her and told her that they were particularly glad that she had come.

"We didn't think you'd come today," said Press, beaming at Iowa as if this day was a special occasion and Iowa the honored guest.

"Why wouldn't I come? I'm always here," she replied, somewhat taken aback by their enthusiasm.

"I don't know. You missed a couple of other days. We're just glad you're here, that's all," added Press, trying not to say anything that might upset her.

"Yes," added Lu, "especially because of what happened."

"You knew about my talk with Ms. Royce?" Iowa didn't immediately understand what Lu had been referring to, but since her talk with Ms. Royce had been the last thing she did before coming to the lake, she naturally assumed that everyone had heard about it and maybe thought it more significant than it really was.

"What? No, I...I mean..." Lu stumbled, reddening in the face because she realized that she had said something she shouldn't have mentioned.

"She means because of the death of your mother," Dana interjected. "I read about it in the paper, and there were a couple of kids talking about it in school. I really don't know why I saw it; I don't like to look at that section of the paper; but for some reason I did, and I'm sorry. It must be hard."

"I'm glad you're here," Luke chimed in. "I heard about it, too, and I can't think of a better place for you to be than here with us – this is where I'd want to be under similar circumstances. I am sorry to hear about your mom."

Everyone was silent for a moment, and each of them – except Luke – appeared uncomfortable, as though someone had said something unpardonable. Except Luke – he smiled slightly, encouragingly, to assuage the sadness that Iowa doubtless felt by the mention of her mother. His smile also had a deeper meaning, although he may not have been entirely aware of it at the time.

Iowa, on the other hand, didn't want to discuss her mother, because as she told them, "It happened, and there's nothing that I can do about it. There are worse things...." She looked across the

shimmering lake when she said that, trying to forget the Smiths
and what was going to happen at the end of the school year.

Everyone was quiet for a few minutes. Like Iowa, each
one was either staring at the surface of the lake or observing the
shore on the other side and, also like Iowa, they were wondering
what to do or say next. Truly, none of them – especially Iowa –
wanted to sit around for the rest of the day moping over a woman
that Iowa herself didn't like (didn't she tell everyone that
hundreds, maybe thousands, of times?) and would have given
"anything" to have lived anywhere except with her? But they
didn't know that Iowa's feelings toward her mother had changed
and that the silence was especially unbearable to her because it
brought up sad memories and regrets that she hadn't been a better
daughter. Press was about to break the oppressive silence by
suggesting they take a stroll through the woods when Iowa
suddenly spoke up and challenged everyone to a game of sticks.

"What about it? I need to get my mind away from my
meeting with Ms. Royce. Do you know what she said this
afternoon?"

Before anyone had a chance to take a stand on sticks, Luke
chimed in and said that he wanted to play that game, too. "You
read my mind," he added.

They all jumped up at the same time and headed for the
woods. For the next ten minutes or so, they scoured the trees and
bushes and the forest floor surrounding them for just the right stick
(among the few, invariable rules of the game were that one had to

choose a different stick for each game and that no stick could be used for more than one game), while keeping an eye out for materials that would enable them to decorate or personalize their sticks. There was no rule that they had to decorate their sticks, but it would have been surprising if they didn't decorate them, since they all compared their sticks before the start of the game to see whose was decorated best. Each stick was generally about three feet long, straight (or reasonably straight), and smooth (small branches, leaves, and, if possible, the bark itself, were removed, leaving a smooth, moist, yellowish rod), while one end was sharpened (not too sharp, however, just enough to look like a point) and the other, which served as a handle, was decorated as elaborately as possible. The materials -- twigs, leaves, long strings of green vines, and so forth -- used for decorations varied with the tastes of the decorators, although none of the Cygnets were averse to sharing their materials, provided that they had extra. The Cygnets returned to the clearing at pretty much the same time and immediately began working on their sticks.

Dana, as she always seemed to do, took a string of leaves and carefully wrapped them around the end of her stick, so that the handle was green and soft, while the very bottom of the handle (the end of the stick) sprouted out a fringe of leaves that were almost all the exact same size and shape. Lu, on the other hand, had collected a smattering of small twigs that she bunched together around the end to thicken it, to give it solidity, and then proceeded to tie the twigs to the end by lacing several strong string-like vines around them and securing them to stick. At either end of what became the handle, she also used the vines to add her own kind of frills or lace-work. Both Press and Luke approached their sticks in a more Spartan-like manner. Press had located some sharp rocks and, after breaking the edges with larger rocks to create a suitable cutting edge, proceeded to notch various shapes and designs into the handle. The shapes and designs, which sometimes bore a resemblance to ancient runes, had no meaning, or so she claimed, other than to display her sense of design when using wedges, gashes, and holes. Luke, though, never considered himself a good designer, and he seemed to lack all but a rudimentary aesthetic sense, and so he contented himself with smoothing both the handle and the rest of his stick, using a rock that, like Press's rock, he made especially for the purpose.

Iowa's stick was different than the others in the way that she used short, curved pieces of wood (these came from a rotting piece of tree, which was easy to cut and shape) to separate the handle from the rest of the stick. The short pieces of wood were fixed to the stick by means of vines and looked remarkably like small wings. Indeed, Iowa stated as much when Press, glancing at what she was doing, asked her how her stick was going and if she wanted to use her "cutter" to help.

"No, thanks," Iowa responded absently, concentrating on her work. "The wood practically crumbles in my hands. Besides, I like the roughness, because it reminds me of feathers."

When done, which took something on the order of fifteen minutes, the Cygnets turned to one another and showed off their sticks. They each took turns holding up their respective stick and showing off the handles and describing what they meant to achieve with their handles. Dana and Lu, for instance, spoke about how they designed handles that were pleasing to the eye, as well as comfortable, which is pretty much what they always said and what they had been saying over the years of playing the game. Dana, in particular, noted the beauty of the leaves and the way they complemented her blouse, which also had ruffles along the edges. No one noticed the repetition of their descriptions, and no one truly cared if they limited themselves to a solitary function instead of doing something different each time. The same was true with Press and Luke, in that they had designed their handles to enable control and grip, which seemed consonant with the views of an athlete and an increasingly rugged boy. Iowa, on the other hand, had usually confined her stick-developing capabilities to broadening the handle, which she usually did by selecting a handful of large twigs and tying them in a bundle to the handle. She often claimed that the twigs absorbed the force from stick itself, which always made one or two of the Cygnets wonder how vigorously she was going to use her stick, which was never very hard. This time, however, she had done nothing with the handle, while the stick itself was thicker to enable her to fasten the wings to it. Her goal, as she said dreamily, looking at the stick and ignoring the Cygnets, was to add swans' wings to her stick, because they would allow her to escape and symbolized the freedom that people lacked, especially at their ages.

"I love swans," she added, looking at the Cygnets as she did so.

Chapter Eight - Next came the rules

Next came the rules. After fashioning their sticks, and before they actually started playing the game, the Cygnets sat down and discussed the rules of the game, going over the game's purpose (that is, what constitutes a win), how to achieve that purpose, and what actions would be considered contrary to the purpose and hence a violation of the rules. This should have been a simple process – after all, they had played the game more times than anyone could remember – but since they never kept records of the rules, and couldn't remember with any certainty how one game differed from another, the rules tended to vary with great regularity each time they played the game. Press, Lu, and Dana all stated, with a great eagerness, that they wanted to "do things a little differently" this time, which only meant that they didn't like something about some previous game and were determined not to repeat it. However, this didn't mean that they all disliked the same something or that this something occurred in the same prior game.

"Let's do this," Press began, as if everyone understood the context that was prompting her ideas.

"We can have two teams, and one person could alternate between the teams as an extra. No, better still, the extra person could be a goalie of some kind…"

"We've done that before," inserted Dana. "You're always the goalie, and nobody has a chance to score."

"Dana's right," Lu added. "You're always the goalie, and your suggestions are always geared toward your strengths. What about the rest of us? I'm not a world-class athlete…"

"Okay, okay," Press said. "What's your brilliant idea?"

Lu hesitated for a moment (the only idea she had was that she didn't want to play by Press's rules). Press was about to press her for an idea – she interpreted Lu's hesitation as confusion and proof that she had nothing to offer -- when Lu perked up and said, "Let's do this." She looked at everyone with a smile, especially Press whom she knew was ready to pounce if she didn't come up with something interesting. "Let's play tag. I know we've done it before, but let's do it this way. We all hide in the woods, and we search out each other to tag them – tap them, Press – with our sticks. One tag equals one point."

"What's so great about…"

"Please, let me finish. One tag equals one point. You have to tag each person twice, and the first person to get to ten points wins."

"So?"

"So," Lu was on a roll, because this seemed like the best idea she had come up with for a very long time. "So, three points against one person doesn't count, and if you get tagged back you lose the point. Every time you're tagged, you lose a point and have to retag the person."

"So if I tag Luke and he tags me back, I lose that point and I need to tag him again to regain my point?" Dana asked to clarify Lu's meaning.

"Yes."

"But then how do you get out of a loop where two of us just stand there and tag each other?

"You can do that if you want to waste time. Remember, the goal is to reach ten points, two points against each person. If you stand there, someone is bound to come up and get their tags against you and win the game. I would suggest that if it looks like you're in a silly loop, then you might as well run to someone else and get a tag and then tag the first person later."

"Okay, but what about teams?" Press asked, now trying to understand the game. "What if two people team up to get more points? It seems like it would easier to win the game that way."

"Not really," replied Dana calmly. The game was beginning to appeal to Dana. "The goal of the game is to have one winner, and so soon or later someone will either have to sacrifice or lose to enable the other to win. It's impossible for more than one person to have ten points, if you lose a point every time you're tagged."

"I get it," said Luke.

Lu pointed to the large rock in the clearing next to edge of the lake. "The first person to score ten points needs to come to the rock and announce it loudly to everyone else. One of the challenges will be to get to the rock without getting tagged.

Remember, the only one going to the clearing will be the person with ten points, which means that if you're nearby, you have a chance to stop that person from winning." Lu looked around at everyone to make sure they understood the rules.

Luke, however, looked puzzled, as if there was now something in the rules that he didn't understand.

"What's your problem?" Press demanded, sounding a little more aggressive than she had intended. She didn't apologize, though, because she was beginning to suspect that Luke was stalling, and there was something about him this day that irritated her. Press adored Luke as much as she adored the other Cygnets, but there were times when he could be exasperating, and it was becoming difficult not to be short with him.

"Well," he began, slowly as if scratching his head over something. Press was convinced that he was being slow on purpose, just to irritate her. "How are we supposed to start? If we start right here, there there's going to be a free-for-all and no one gets anywhere."

"Good point," said Lu.

"Let's count to twenty and then start," Press interjected. "That will give everyone time to get a good position before beginning." She turned to Luke. "And no peeking, otherwise you lose a point."

Luke smiled in agreement, but didn't respond. He realized that sometimes it was best not to respond to Press, especially when matters of competition were concerned.

"Two," Lu added, not to be shut out of the discussion. Since the rules were her idea, Lu had positioned herself in the center of the clearing and was ready to begin counting when Iowa suddenly charged out and, slashing her stick at Lu's, which she had been holding upright, knocked it out of her hands.

"One point," Iowa called out as she ran to the trees.

"That's not fair," Lu cried after her, picking her stick off the ground at the same time. "You didn't get a point because I didn't finish counting." But before she could holler out a single number, the others took Iowa's lead and ran into the woods, too, each in a different direction. "That's cheating. You're all cheaters," cried Lu, as she, too, ran into the woods.

The sun was descending and casting deep shadows across the trees. Although it was still light enough to see the trees, the fields, and the lake clearly, the ground was getting darker and the undergrowth between the trees was losing its color and becoming gray and gloomy. Before the Cygnets ran toward the trees, everything seemed draped with a hush that was broken only by the occasional caw and the creaking of tired tree limbs overhead as they rocked from a gentle breeze touching their tops. Once the Cygnets entered the woods, however, the sounds of their feet crashing through the undergrowth seemed to echo from all directions, and squeals and laughter bounced off the trees as the Cygnets ran for cover or tagged one another.

Within seconds, Lu had been tagged three times (once by Iowa, which she continued to protest, and twice by Dana), and so in frustration she decided to hide for a few minutes to keep from being tagged anymore. Remembering the large outcrop near the clearing, she immediately dashed through the woods toward the rocks, which, because they were surrounded by trees, she reasonably expected would keep her safe from the others, at least for a while. As soon as she reached it, Lu clambered up between two big boulders and then settled into the narrow crevasse between them. From this position, she could peek over the lower boulder in front of her to track anyone venturing nearby, while remaining practically invisible unless they were practically in front of her.

Press was moving in the opposite direction. Like Lu, she sought a place where she could hide from the others. But unlike the other girl, Press wanted to find a good place where she could track the others without being observed and, when the time was right, attack them from behind, hopefully scoring points without losing any in return. Having roamed the woods for years, Press quickly realized that the best hiding place anyone could have would be high up in the trees, because it was hard to see anything among the leaves (and, realistically, who would look up expecting to find anyone, especially when they were tromping through dense, sometimes uncertain, undergrowth?) and because you could observe a much greater area than when you were on the ground. Press selected a particularly tall tree with lots of thick, leafy branches and scampered up maybe ten feet to a thick branch that offered excellent views of both the area beneath the tree and, between a couple of smaller, barren trees in front, a sizeable portion of the lake, particularly the rock in the clearing where the winner could announce victory. Settling down on the branch, Press leaned against the fat trunk of the tree and, after tucking one leg beneath her and letting the other dangle midair, she began to scan the woods and the clearing for any signs of the others.

Calm, and pleased with her hiding spot, Press waited for the others who sooner or later would have to pass somewhere near the tree. Pleased as well by her wise choice of trees, she looked carefully around the base of the tree (her view from this perspective was limited because of the thickness of the tree and because she didn't immediately check out the area behind her back) and, after finding nothing amiss, out to the edge of the lake and the rock, which inexplicably seemed in need of protection. The ambient noise was even more inexplicable. While Press had half-expected to be surrounded by complete silence this high up, no sooner than she settled in and began looking for the Cygnets than she noticed the cacophony of sounds that floated and swirled all around her. She had climbed trees before and been even higher than she was now, but she had never noticed the whoosh of the breeze as it whipped in and out of the branches, or the leaves, which rattled like the applause of a large, appreciative audience. And then there were the creaks and groans from the trees themselves, which from time to time would turn into a large snap as a branch lost its hold on a distant tree and crashed down to the ground, where it was engulfed in darkness among the welcoming undergrowth.

Motionless and practically holding her breath, Press tried to appropriate the skills that her white Persian cat, Charles, used to capture a mouse on the garage or a sparrow in the back yard. But after a while – and especially after her foot, which had been neatly placed beneath her, started to become uncomfortable and then hurt as sharp edges of bark poked her flesh – she started to consider the disadvantages of being so high off the ground. If, for example, she spotted someone approaching the tree, it was quite likely that this person would be long gone by the time Press climbed down or dropped out of the tree (even though she had little fear of heights, ten feet -- or however far down it was to the base of the tree – did seem to be a little too far to fall and remain unhurt). Moreover, if she was noticed descending, her intended victim might very well have enough time to deliver a couple of neat tags to her backside and escape before she had a chance to respond. Of course, the only Cygnets with that much speed and agility were Luke and Iowa, which was irksome because she didn't know where they were – or indeed where any of the other Cygnets were.

Given her increasing suspicions that she was vulnerable in the tree, Press rose onto her feet, climbed down to another branch a couple feet closer to the ground, and, positioning herself so that one arm wrapped around the tree's trunk and her free hand grasped a slight branch above her for balance, she took in every sight and sound that might reveal the presence of the others. From her position, she seemed especially sensitive to the sounds floating among the bushes and leaves. If a branch landed on the soft ground nearby, Press turned her head quickly in the direction of the thud, trying to figure out if it was indeed a branch or someone nearby; and if the breeze came up and rattled the leaves below her, she twisted her body in the direction of the rattling, listening intently for the Cygnet who might have ducked around the bushes to avoid being spotted. Once, after she had been holding still for about five minutes, Press caught wind of a series of regular, though faintly audible thuds, which, because of their regularity, could only have come from one of the Cygnets trying to sneak up on her. She couldn't see anyone approaching, however, and so she began to suspect that they might be crawling through the foliage on the ground to disguise their presence. Squinting, Press visually examined every nook and cranny, checked the tops of the bushes for signs of movement caused by someone maneuvering underneath them, until the muscles in her eyes were sore and she was forced to admit that no one was there – and she shook her head in disgust when she realized that the muffled thuds were not emanating from somewhere on the ground but from her own chest, her heart beating loudly in anticipation of action.

Since it was now clear that no one was nearby, at least not directly in front of the tree, Press carefully maneuvered around the tree trunk to get a better look at the other side of the woods, but no sooner had she rounded the tree and settled on another large branch than she caught sight of something unexpected and unwelcome. In a tall tree maybe twenty feet away, Dana was looking directly at Press. She was slightly below Press's line of sight and standing, holding a branch, in much the same manner as Press (if Dana had physically resembled Press in any way, Press might have considered the possibility that she was looking into a mirror). Instead of jumping down, Press didn't move and couldn't help thinking that Dana must have climbed her tree at exactly the same instant that Press climbed hers, for there was no other way she could explain how Dana had scaled the tree without Press noticing it or hearing the noise. For a few moments, neither one of them could do nothing but stare at one another – Press surprised that Dana was there, and Dana surprised that Press had noticed her – but when these moments had passed, Dana was the first to react.

Quicker witted than Press, Dana suddenly turned, slipped down into a seated position on the branch, and maneuvered her body so that her stomach straddled the branch while her hands held snugly on the branch to prevent her from falling off. Press was surprised at Dana's agility and athletic prowess – she would never have believed that the girl could be so flexible and sure in her movements – especially when she flipped over the branch until she was hanging by her hands and, a fraction of a second later, dropped to the soft undergrowth below. Luckily, Dana only had about four feet to drop, and so she was able to land on her feet, albeit so unsteadily that she dropped to the seat of her pants, unhurt, of course. Press continued to watch in amazement as Dana jumped up and took off, running away from the tree and toward the rocky outcrop. Once Dana was out of sight, Press realized that she was no longer safe from tagging, and she too descended the tree and, remaining on her feet when she hit the ground, started after Dana, whom she was certain that she could catch and tag quite easily. Dana knew that Press would be following her, so she charged forward, jumping bushes and bounding around other obstacles. She didn't know where she was going, only that she needed to get away from Press as quickly as possible – there was no evading Press's long, athletic strides. Rounding a large tree, Dana came face to face with an obstruction that sent her once again onto the seat of her pants.

Dana had swung around the tree just as Luke was coming around from the opposite side, and their collision sent Dana to the ground. Luke staggered slightly, but being more than a head taller than Dana and considerably heavier and more muscular, he had little trouble remaining on his feet.

Slightly dazed, both were initially a little foggy regarding the impact and its cause, but as soon as Luke noticed Dana sitting on the ground with her legs stretched out in front of her, and her arms and hands behind her back and propping up her shoulders and chest, he grasped what had happened and immediately reached down to help her up. "Gosh, I'm sorry, Dana. I didn't see…are you okay? Are you hurt?"

Dana shook her head slowly. She felt a little lightheaded, but as she looked up at Luke looming just in front of her, she too began to understand why she was on the seat of her pants. "No,

I'm fine," she replied, and then laughed a little while shaking her head. "Fancy meeting you here," she added with a smile.

"Are you sure you're okay?" Luke asked, genuinely concerned that he may have hurt her. When she affirmed that she was unhurt, Luke breathed a sigh of relief and then tagged her twice with his stick. "That's two. See ya later, gator," he shouted and ran off, disappearing in the trees behind her.

Mad that she had allowed Luke to tag her without getting even, Dana brushed the dust off the seat of her pants and turned toward the outcrop. She wasn't going to follow Luke to take back the hits, since he was too fast and already had an insurmountable lead. However, because she now expected Press to be coming her way, Dana didn't hesitate for a second more and began to run as fast as she could, filling her lungs with deep gulps of reinvigorating air. But before she had traveled twenty feet, Press appeared seemingly out of nowhere and delivered two quick hits.

"That's two for me," Press hollered, as she, too, disappeared in the trees, although in a different direction than Luke.

Dana turned and ran after Press. But because she was no match for Press either, she quickly fell behind and soon lost track of her altogether. Her side aching and her lungs pleading for air, Dana slowed and then stopped, bending over and breathing deeply to recuperate. When she felt better, she straightened up and looked up and down the path, which was the same path that led from the neighborhood to the lake and back again. Nobody was in sight, and there wasn't a single sound to suggest that anyone was nearby, not even Press or Luke. With the light beginning to dim, Dana decided to head toward the lake to see if she could find someone and determine if the game was still going on, or if anyone had gone home.

Dana was within sight of the lake when she heard some rustling in the trees ahead, after which someone shouted "Tag!" Knowing that she was vulnerable on the path, she stepped off the path and trotted through the undergrowth to the outcrop, which she was certain would give her cover and a place from which to find the others. As soon as she reached the rocks, she began to climb – first, on a series of small ledges that, like steps, led to a broader ledge, which itself led, at a sixty-degree angle, to the second highest rise of the outcrop – and once on top, she stood upright for a few seconds to see where everyone was. In the distance, to her left, she could hear some shouting, the rustling of the undergrowth, but she still couldn't see anyone. Dana was about to climb down on the other side of the outcrop when she noticed, just over the edge, Lu still hiding in the crevasse.

It was startling to have come upon the other girl so unexpectedly, since she had no idea that anyone was close. Her surprise dissipated quickly and nearly turned to outright laughter when she realized that Lu hadn't heard her scaling the rocks and was, in fact, unaware of her presence overhead a few feet away. Not wanting to lose a great opportunity, Dana stifled her chuckles and backed quietly away from the ledge and then climbed down the rocks, after which she snuck around the back of the outcrop to Lu's hiding place, where the girl was still lying still and looking in the opposite direction. Two rock steps and she was within reach of Lu's shoes and, carefully reaching out with her stick, she slapped the bottoms of Lu's shoes.

"That's one," Dana cried as she jumped down onto the ground, followed by Lu scrambling after her.

At almost the very instant Lu touched the ground, Press appeared from the other side of the outcrop and tapped her on the back. Press would have cried tag, but Lu was too quick and no sooner had she been tagged than she twirled around and tagged Press, hollering, "Doesn't count." Press managed to retag Lu and, at the same time, avoid being retagged as she jumped back to avoid Lu's fruitless effort and ran away, hollering, "Does too."

Press was again moving too quickly to pursue, but as Lu turned around to determine what to do next, she spotted Dana, who had been watching Lu and Press exchange tags. Startled out of her reverie, Dana turned, stumbled slightly in the undergrowth, and took off, with Lu in hot pursuit.

Chapter Nine - Iowa had run from the lake into a section of the woods

Iowa had run from the lake into a section of the woods where no one, she was certain, would think to find her. When she slapped Lu's stick and ran away, everyone thought that she was being playful and eager to start the game; she may have been a little rough, but with games like this one it is sometimes easy to get a little carried away. At least, that's what most of them thought. Iowa, however, wasn't certain about her own thoughts, because something inside her wanted to strike out at Lu, to punish the girl for no other reason than for being Lu, although she would never have tried to hurt her physically – such a thought would never have occurred to Iowa. Iowa loved Lu as much as she loved the others, but she couldn't help teasing the girl from time to time, doing almost anything simply to get a rise out of her, after which she would shower her with apologies and do her best to mollify her. Iowa couldn't explain her behavior, she couldn't explain why getting a rise out of the poor girl could sometimes be fun (and Iowa would have defended Lu to the death had anyone other than a Cygnet touched her), but she did it all the same and Lu had come to expect it, sometimes even appearing to appreciate the humor in it. This time, though, while it may have seemed just another instance of Iowa needling Lu, Iowa was not playing one of her cruel games but was actually acting in anger – she wanted to insult Lu, she wanted the girl to feel her disdain, but not to the degree that anyone else would notice and think less of her because of it.

Sitting comfortably on the ground, her back against a large tree and waist-high bushes surrounding and concealing her, Iowa mulled over what had happened, feeling increasingly sad and empty because she had hurt one of her best friends. She couldn't fathom why she had behaved this way – and Lu wasn't the only person whom Iowa had treated in such a mean fashion – and she didn't completely understand why she had been feeling restless and angry with almost everyone, especially people who wanted to change and control her life (maybe it was Lu's silly rules that elicited Iowa's reaction). But as she considered the things that were happening in her life, she quickly came to realize that the Smiths were the root of all her problems – the Smiths, who promised to remove her from school and friends, were tearing her up inside and forcing her to respond in a way that was generally uncharacteristic of her. It was the Smiths, there was no doubt about it, and even though life now seemed a little clearer because of this realization, it didn't change anything – it didn't solve the problem of what to do in response. Iowa wasn't going to go with the Smiths, but at the moment that was the only thing she could say with any certainty. Moreover, it didn't solve the problem of Lu and how she was going to make it up to her this time or, for that matter, stop this stupid game. Normally, Iowa would have loved a game of sticks, even if the rules changed each time it was played, but in her present mood, and feeling increasingly guilty over what she had done to Lu, she hated the game, hated running around and being forced to do something that now seemed stupid and pointless. The only thing she wanted now was to sit and watch the gentle swaying of the treetops, which were pushed this way and that by the overhead breezes.

Luckily, no one seemed within earshot, and it was unlikely that any of them would be looking for her, since it was getting late and the game, if it was not already over (sitting in her retreat, Iowa had lost track of time), would likely be winding down. But Iowa was fully prepared to sit there all night – watching the trees and then, as the sky turned black and small, pinpoint pricks of light danced across her field of vision, observing the progression of the moon as it emerged from the forest on the left, migrated across the night sky toward the right, and fell back among the trees – when she noticed the faint sounds of footsteps slowly and carefully moving nearby, perhaps only a few feet away. Slowing her breathing so that she would not be detected, Iowa reached into the bushes and carefully parted a handful of the branches to see who might be nearby and to determine if they were looking for her. Unfortunately, it was difficult, if not impossible, to see anything clearly through the bushes except through one small opening near the ground (the bushes were dead and leafless there). Bending over – moving slowly and quietly so as not to rustle so much as a leaf that might signal her presence – and placing her ear next to a barren patch of dirt at the base of the bushes, Iowa was able to see a small section of the path near her tree. This section was too small to identify anyone (she could only see from the ground up to about six inches), although it was enough to see the shoes of someone close and, if these shoes had hesitated, quite possibly to determine if the owner was listening and searching for someone. And just as she positioned herself perfectly to identify the presence of someone near, everything became silent and she could neither hear nor see anything indicating the presence of another human being.

Not convinced that the person was gone, Iowa continued to listen intently and did her best to scan quietly the area visible through her peephole. Pushing her cheek deeper into the soft dirt and practically poking her nose through the bushes, she tried to extract as much information as she possible could through these limited means; and because her little area was too narrow and confined to allow her to stretch out and look up through the peephole, she was forced to position herself on her knees, the tops of her legs tight against her chest, while the side of her head was on the ground. Iowa remained in this position for several minutes, her muscles aching and dirt filling her nose, but she refused to relax and make her presence known. It had ceased long ago to be a matter of playing the game and eluding her competitors; instead, she was increasingly determined to evade the Cygnets and everyone else so that she would concentrate and figure out what to do next – and what to do next was wrapped up in evading the

Smith's clutches. 'What can I do?' she asked herself while looking through the bushes. 'Maybe I'll run away. Maybe…,' she began to consider when she felt two sharp stabs against her backside and, immediately afterwards, heard Luke bellow, "Got you! Two points!" Even before she had a chance to stand up and respond, she could hear Luke running off and crashing through the undergrowth. Furious that Luke had violated her privacy with his stupid game, Iowa jumped up, tore through her enclosure, and took off in pursuit of Luke.

Luke had a good head start, but Iowa was able to keep pace with him, never falling more than ten or fifteen feet behind him. Indeed, there were times when she seemed to be gaining on him, particularly when he had to leap an obstruction or round a sharp corner – and during these moments she closed within inches of being able to grab his shirt, the tails of which floated behind him like ragged sails on a boat. At one point, Luke stumbled over a large tree root and nearly fell down, enabling Iowa to touch his shirt, but she couldn't quite get close enough to grab it because she, too, stumbled over the same root and, unlike Luke, actually fell down, her chin, arms, and chest sliding into the dirt. She jumped up immediately and, without checking herself, continued her pursuit – now angry that it was she and not Luke who had fallen, and furious that it was her clothes and not Luke's that were dirty and probably torn. And Iowa promised herself to hold Luke responsible if she skinned anything in the fall.

Luke had for a moment or two followed the path, but he suddenly veered off and began running through the woods, dodging trees and leaping over fallen branches, bounding through the undergrowth, and sometimes grabbing a tree trunk and using his strength to swing around the tree and veer off into another direction. This tactic only added to Iowa's fire, because he did it time after time; and no matter how hard Iowa tried to emulate his actions, she could never grasp the tree tightly enough and would either swing too widely and hence fall behind or lose her grip altogether and fall down. If that wasn't bad enough, Luke appeared to be doing these things to make fun of her – why else would he be swinging around the trees so often, and why did he continue to look back at her and smile? In fact, what angered Iowa most was that Luke kept looking back at her, confident, often smiling, and never once appeared concerned that she might catch up with him. Even when she closed the gap between them, she wasn't entirely certain that she was truly catching up as opposed to Luke slowing down and allowing her to get within reach of his shirt tails, only to speed off the instance she reached out to grab them. Indeed, the last time she stumbled while following him around a tree, he seemed to slow significantly until she was up and, once again, charging after him. He had to be playing with her – he had to be! – but unfortunately there was no way that she could pay him back for his efforts, not until he stopped, and he didn't seem to want to stop.

Unexpectedly, Luke left the trees and began running through the tall grasses that in some places lined the woods, and just as unexpectedly he returned to the woods and began running as if he was heading to a particular destination. Iowa followed, determined not to give up – never to give up, or at least never to give up to Luke – and together, Luke first by about ten feet, and then Iowa, they went over one small hill after another until they were in sight of the outcrop. No one else was visible, and Luke headed for the outcrop, rounding one corner of a large, rectangular boulder and then disappearing altogether. Iowa followed him around the corner, and then the next corner and the next, without once spotting him. She couldn't believe that she had lost him so quickly. She couldn't believe that he had vanished around a single corner. Stopping and catching her breath, she turned around several times, glancing at the base of the outcrop and then the fields. When this proved fruitless, she ran to another side of the rocks and surveyed the outcrop and the fields in that direction. Had he truly disappeared, had she been chasing a ghost? Embarrassed that she had lost him, she stood still with her fists at her waist, listening for clues that he might be nearby, or even that any of the other Cygnets might be within shouting distance.

Iowa was ready to give up and return to the vicinity of the lake, when she heard her name being called. At first, she couldn't tell in which direction the sound emanated – it was soft and sounded far away – and, in fact, she wasn't completely certain that it was her name that was being called. But after a few moments, the sound kept repeating until it was clear that it was indeed her name, even if the direction was still muddled. After a few moments of this, Iowa was ready to leave and forget both Luke and the voice when a voice overhead called her name loudly and clearly: "Iowa!" It was Luke, and he had been standing on top of the outcrop, obviously following her movements and reveling in her foolishness.

"It's your conscience, Iowa. How come you didn't look up?" Luke was standing a few feet out of reach, and not only were his arms arrogantly folded, but he was also smiling and laughing – barely able to speak because of his laughter – and all at her expense. She couldn't stand it.

Running toward a section of the outcrop that led to the top where Luke was standing, Iowa charged madly up the rocks, injuring her fingertips in the process but more determined than ever to get Luke once and for all. Slipping and scrambling, she made it to the top just as Luke, smiling at her as she stood up, turned around and leaped the ground. He fell on one knee but, unhurt, he jumped up and started across the field and headed into the trees toward the lake. Iowa, despite her anger and desire to catch Luke, couldn't make the leap and so she scampered down the same way she came up. She didn't lose sight of Luke, however, because he was waiting for her just inside the woods and, when she was within ten feet, turned and headed again toward the lake.

Luke jumped over roots and bushes, stumbled on stumps, rocks, and inexplicable holes, and somehow managed to remain upright as he ran, staying comfortably ahead of Iowa, who was becoming increasingly tired, her lungs demanding a rest. Feeling sorry for her, and wishing that she would catch and tag him, Luke slowed as he arrived at the clearing and then the inexplicable happened – Luke tripped over a soft spot in the earth just inside the clearing and fell face forward onto the open ground. Just then the others arrived, having seen the arrival of Luke and then Iowa and assuming that Luke had won the game.

Breathing heavily, Iowa walked slowly over to where Luke laid, face down, his head resting on his cradled arms, and stopped. She bent over for a few moments trying to recover her breath, which during those moments seemed an impossible task, but when she finally recovered somewhat, she took a couple of steps closer to the boy. Luke hadn't moved. Clearly, he, too, was winded, but unlike Iowa he needed only to lie down and relax. Iowa, feeling a little better, stared at him intently for nearly a minute, obviously tossing something around in her mind, and then tagged him twice in the same area that he had tagged her, only much harder than he had hit her. "Tag," she gasped, suddenly out of breath again. Her face was red and sweaty – she was still far from recovered – and for a moment it looked like she was going to say something to Luke, but didn't. She stepped back and again bent forward, this time grabbing her right side. A strange, throbbing pain emanated from inside her side, but there was nothing she could do except stop and wait for the pain to subside, waiting as well for her breathing to slow down and for the rest of her body to return to its normal state (she was surprised at how tired she now felt).

Naturally, she blamed Luke for how she felt. In fact, for a few moments, she told herself that she hated Luke – she hated him for spying on her, for tagging her when she couldn't defend herself (and tagging her on her rear end, of all things), for forcing her to expend an enormous amount of energy on this stupid game, and for ruining her clothes. She could see the dirt on the front of her pants, and she noticed out of the corner of one eye (she didn't want to turn her head because others would notice) that the sleeve of her blouse was ripped, probably from one of the falls in the forest. But she was mad at the others, too, because everyone was standing around quietly, neither intervening nor commiserating with her over her exhaustion or the state of her clothes – and, as she rolled all this around in her mind, she became upset with everything and everyone else, too. In normal families, children can go to their parents to heal their injuries, to buy them new clothes, and to make sure that things like this never happen, or at least never happen again. But not her; the Cygnets were uncaring, her parents had never been normal, and now she was stuck with the Smiths, who were not only weird, but who were also ugly, crude, and embarrassing. Luke, while he might not have been responsible for the Smiths, rubbed her nose in the fact that his parents were normal – he loved his parents, and he didn't mind telling Iowa and the rest of the Cygnets about this singular fact. Not surprisingly, these and some other unpleasant thoughts began to pass from Iowa's mind as the pain in her side subsided, and she might even have become sorry for having thought about Luke in this way had it not been for the way he was now looking at her.

Luke stood up. It was obvious he wasn't hurt and, if she hadn't seen him fall, Iowa would have been hard pressed to identify anything on him or his clothes that suggested he had been running through bushes and had fallen, face first, on the ground. He wasn't even breathing heavily. But instead of saying anything or trying to retag Iowa, Luke stood motionlessly. He could feel a slight breeze come up from the left, and as he looked at Iowa's dour face, he thought it was the most beautiful face he had ever seen, especially as the dying light made the side of her face glow and the breeze kept forcing long strands of her hair across her face, which she kept pushing back. For a brief moment, he could see himself stepping over to her, brushing her hair out of her eyes, and touching her face with the tips of his fingers. Of course, he would never take such a step without a clear indication that Iowa desired it, but the thought that she might somehow ask him to do so forced a slight, involuntary smile to crease his lips and made his hand loosened its grip on the stick, allowing it to fall almost noiselessly to the ground.

Iowa looked at Luke and then, for some reason, at her stick. She was surprised that the wings had fallen off and, glancing at the ground and seeing nothing but dirt and rocks, it was obvious that they had fallen off sometime during the wild goose chase that Luke had engineered. Without wings, the stick was just a stick, and all her efforts at taking an ordinary stick and making it a thing of beauty were lost, languishing somewhere among the weeds and dirt in the woods. As much as she wanted to think nice thoughts about everybody, Iowa couldn't help blaming Luke for this, too, for if he hadn't taunted her and forced her to chase him, the stick would have remained intact and one of the few beautiful objects left in her life. Why did he have to do it, she thought, why did he have to spy on her, hit her with his stick, and then challenge her to a chase that he knew would cause endless problems for both of them? What was the matter with him? And why was he smiling? Why was he always smiling when he looked at her? Why was he always looking at her? She didn't like it, and she didn't like him, of all people, doing it. These and a plethora of other thoughts began flying through her mind, and instead of opening her mouth and speaking to the boy, instead of trying to defuse her rising anger – anger, which deep down she knew had no sound or legitimate basis – she stood silently and let everything come to a head. For one brief second, it appeared that Luke might say something, but before he could open his mouth, Iowa grasped her stick tightly and, with a flick that was too quick to duck, hit him solidly under the left eye. By pure chance it missed his eye – she didn't know why, but she had aimed for his eye – but it caused a rapidly-rising welt and a trickle of blood to run down his cheek.

"Ow," Luke cried out and, bending at the waist, covered his eye with both of his hands. For a moment, it certainly appeared that she had hit his eye, but when he removed his hands to look up at her, visually asking her why she had hit him, it was clear that his eye was unscathed.

That may not have mattered, however, because for a few seconds Iowa didn't care if his eye was hurt or not. She didn't follow this strike with another, nor did she attempt even the vaguest apology. She stood watching at him as if his efforts to ease the pain under his eye were his business and that she was the last person to interfere with someone else's business. It was also the case that she couldn't help wondering why he didn't do anything as a result, other than rub his eye and try to hide his tears. He didn't even demand an answer to her actions. He just stood there, refusing to do anything in response, refusing even to step back in case she tried to hit him again. This, too, irritated her, and she felt disgusted by his weak or inexplicable behavior.

Luke had no intention of backing away. He was shocked by Iowa's behavior, he had done nothing to provoke what was obviously a mean-spirited act, and his feelings were hurt because she was a friend who had discarded his friendship like one discards a pair of old shoes. He should have walked away, but for some reason he stood his ground, calmly, painfully, but without anger.

The others were taken aback by this strange and unprecedented act, and they quickly converged on Luke to see if he was okay. Luke wiped the blood and tears from his eye, and he tried to act as if the hit didn't hurt and Iowa wasn't to be blamed (or not very much) for what she had done. "It was an accident," he said when the others, standing beside Luke, turned toward Iowa, horrified that she had done something like this to a fellow Cygnet.

"Accident?" one of them groaned.

Chapter Ten - "What's the matter with you?"

"What's the matter with you?" Lu cried out, alternately looking at Iowa and at Luke, holding his eye.

"You're bleeding," Dana added, as if she alone had noticed this obvious fact (the edge of his hand was red with smeared blood).

Press stepped over to Luke and, pulling his hand away from his eye, examined the injury very carefully. Since she was an athlete, she had seen numerous sports injuries and so she felt qualified to examine the eye and pronounce judgment. Poking the quickly-rising lump, and wiping away small spots of blood that kept rising beneath his eye, she stated authoritatively that "the eye" was fine, although he could have been blinded very easily (she said this while glancing over her left shoulder at Iowa). "You need to wash the area when you get home and put some ice on it to reduce the swelling," she said, remembering all the cuts and bruises she had suffered in competition. Standing back and away from Luke, she turned to Iowa and demanded to know what had happened, as if she didn't know and was trying to catch Iowa in a lie.

Iowa didn't respond, and for a few seconds didn't move or turn away from Luke. Luke was the first to move. He wiped the blood from his cheek with the back of his hand, and then stepped away from the girls and stood close to Iowa's side. Smiling pleasantly and looking at Press, Dana, and Lu, he stated that nothing had happened. "I'm afraid it was my fault," he said, trying to act like one of the characters he had seen on a TV show. He hesitated while all eyes were on him, including Iowa's, and added for good measure, "I'm sorry. I didn't mean to sound so dramatic."

"I'm not surprised," said Press. "It's a terrible injury. Maybe we should take you home to see if someone needs to take you to the doctor." The other girls, except Iowa, seconded Press's idea and competed among themselves to see who would take the responsibility of seeing him home.

Iowa stepped back, and walked over to a log that was only about ten feet or so from the path that led out of the park.

"What's the matter with you?" Dana inquired, curious about her friend's strange, aloof behavior. The other girls and Luke looked over at Iowa. "You of all people should want to help."

"Nothing is the matter with me," Iowa said defensively. "And why should I want to help? It was an accident, you heard him. It's not serious; he's going to heal, and so what's the big deal?"

There was silence for a moment, as if none of them could understand their friend's cavalier attitude and lack of responsibility.

"I can't believe you. You don't mean that," Lu replied softly, breaking the silence.

"I don't care if you believe me or not. And who gave you the right to tell me what I mean?"

"I only meant…"

Luke quickly intervened when he saw Lu back away and tears begin to well in her eyes. Lu didn't like confrontations, especially with her closest friends.

"It's okay," he said to everyone, not looking at Iowa. "It's fine. I'm not hurt, at least not bad enough to call a doctor. My mom can wash it up tonight. And Iowa's right, it wasn't her fault and she doesn't need to offer an apology or anything like that. I…ah…you didn't see it, but I moved forward just as she was going to tag me again. So you see, I accidently poked myself. But it's nothing. It's not worth all this commotion."

Everyone was silent and, again, they looked at Luke and then Iowa and back again.

"Are you kidding me?" Press asked, her mouth slightly open.

"Of course, not," Luke said with a big smile on his lips, at the same time continuing to wipe the blood from his cheek. By now a rather sizeable lump had risen beneath his eye, although it didn't appear that it would affect his eyesight. He could feel the swelling and, even though it throbbed, it wasn't that painful, and he couldn't help wondering if it had been painful enough to warrant the yell and the tears. "It's okay," added for good measure, and then turned to Iowa. "It was my fault, wasn't it, Iowa?"

He really didn't know what he could gain from such a statement, but it made him feel somewhat gallant by enlisting Iowa in his lie, as if perhaps she would be grateful to him because of his actions. He was disabused of this notion quickly enough when she looked at him and then everyone else, after which she threw down her stick and began walking toward the path.

"What's the matter with you?" they called after her, although none of them attempted to follow her and keep her with the group. "Iowa?"

The girls again clustered around Luke, while he watched Iowa walk away from the lake. The game was over, and no one felt like playing a new game or doing much of anything else. Sitting down on the grass and logs, they chatted aimlessly for a few minutes trying not to mention what had happened. The sun had finally disappeared and a cool breeze was picking up, rattling the leaves and creating small whitecaps on the lake. When Luke mentioned that his eye was beginning to hurt and that he needed to go home, they all got up more or less at the same time and followed him along the path and out of the park. Everyone was silent. No one said anything to Luke; and, while they were silent about Iowa's inexplicable behavior, they couldn't help wondering what had actually happened and why she was so angry with Luke. Luke, too, had wondered about her behavior, and it hurt him more than his injury because it was obvious that she didn't like him, at least not like she used to.

Iowa didn't come to the lake the following day, and she wasn't at school throughout the week that followed.

Chapter Eleven - The Smiths didn't know where Iowa was

The Smiths didn't know where Iowa was either. When Iowa didn't come home the following day, the Smiths called the police and reported her as a runaway. The police, overburdened as they often are, told the Smiths that they would keep an eye out for the girl, but they added that there are a lot of runaways these days and it wouldn't be surprising if she showed up the next day, hungry and sorry that she had left such loving parents. When asked what anyone could do, the police emphasized that they would watch for her, but that they didn't have the resources to track down runaways. "Try a friend or someone she knows," they added, "because the kids tend to go to familiar places rather than risk sleeping in alleys or in fields."

"What if she had been abducted," Mrs. Smith practically cried in the phone.

"If you have evidence to that fact, Ma'am, then we'll report it as an abduction and start the procedures for tracking down the child. But it is pointless to suggest it at this point unless you have some facts we can act on. Are there facts to suggest this?" When she said no, he added that there was every reason to expect her back in a day or so, when she realizes how good she had it at home. "However, let us know immediately if anything new comes up."

The Smiths were naturally distraught, especially since they felt that they were letting Iowa's mother down. She had entrusted them with her only child, and now the only child was gone, lost, somewhere out of their control and their ability to protect and guide her. "Who knows," Mr. Smith bellowed, "who knows what she could be getting into. And those friends of hers…well, I never liked them, and I like them even less now." Mr. Smith was sitting in a large, vinyl-covered lounger that he had brought with them to Iowa's mother's house. Leaning back, his arms crossed across his enormous stomach, he stared at a blank TV screen while he attended to Mrs. Smith's words.

Mrs. Smith stood at his side and looked directly him while she spoke. "But we've never met them, dear."

"I don't care, but when I find out who they are, I am going to speak to their parents and make sure they never see Iowa again. And I'll tell you one more thing, my dear, there are going to be some changes around here when she gets back."

"What do you mean?"

Without changing his position, Mr. Smith turned his head toward his wife and looked at her sternly, the corners of his full lips turned downward, as if she herself were in some kind of trouble. He tapped his temple several times with his left hand, as if he were thinking of something very important, and then spoke calmly but firmly. "I mean enough of this pussyfooting around just because her parents are gone. I mean we are going to have some structure in life, not like it is now, not like it used to be. I mean we are going home as soon as possible. She will get the proper instruction there, and in short order she will become a well-mannered, useful citizen."

"Yes, of course, but aren't you forgetting that we agreed to allow her to finish the term here before moving? It would be so disruptive to move now. I know how you feel about her friends, but maybe it's a good thing they're around to help her get over the loss of her mother. Maybe…"

"Maybe, but I'm not going to tolerate this nonsense anymore." Mr. Smith sat up, although neither his arms nor the corners of his mouth changed positions. "I didn't pull any of this nonsense when I was her age, and neither did you, my dear. We behaved properly; we did what we were told. And now it's going to be the same here…or…or we'll leave a lot sooner than she expects."

Mrs. Smith walked across the room to the sofa that was directly across from Mr. Smith. Brushing some crumbs off before submitting her dress to the fabric, Mrs. Smith eased her large body onto the soft cushion and looked directly at her husband, waiting for his next pronouncement. She didn't have to wait long, for once she appeared comfortable, Mr. Smith, who had been following her movements with great interest, began speaking as if he had something in the back of his mind, some plan or stratagem, that he had planned to share with his wife at exactly the right moment.

"And I'll tell you another thing. This animal business, it's going to stop now. Do you understand me?"

"Of course, I do." Mrs. Smith hesitated for a moment. Standing up and smoothing out her dress, she stepped over to Mr. Smith, and holding out her right hand, silently invited him to stand up and grasp her hand. When he did so, not without several loud grunts as if the exertion required to stand was physically taxing, Mrs. Smith led him to the sofa and, after letting him settle into the thick cushions, sat down next to him. She pulled his giant arm over her shoulder and snuggled next to him.

"I agree," she said quietly. "It was different with us, but Iowa never got the attention from her father that she should have. Her mother told me that many times. He was so obsessed with his animal nature it took control of the human part of him and…well, neither his mind nor his body was strong enough to handle the changes. We see it all the time. It certainly isn't new."

"He was a weakling."

"Yes, dear, he was, unlike you and her mother. I realize we didn't know her very well, but I am beginning to miss her. She wasn't like most of the people we help. She truly understood the temptations, and so she was able to craft a fairly reasonable life for herself and her child. Don't you think that's so? And don't you think that's rare? I mean, how many people do we see in any given year that are like her?"

"Do you think she said anything to the girl?" Mr. Smith angled his head downward and looked at his wife. "I believe the papers noted that the girl witnessed the father's change on his deathbed, but I don't think there was anything in there about what the mother may have said to her. I don't want to look now, but do you remember if she ever said anything to the girl?"

"I don't know, dear. She learned something from either her father or her mother, otherwise the woman wouldn't have given us a call. However, I think we should keep it to ourselves when she comes back, because it might stir up her desires…"

"Her desires?" he interrupted, turning his face away from her and looking at the wall across the room. "She may be acting out her desires right now, for all we know. But when she comes back, we'll find out – and then there'll be some changes."

"I hope we don't have to be harsh. Maybe it would be worthwhile speaking to her teacher, Ms. Royce.

"We can handle this by ourselves. We are not at the point in which we need outside help."

"I'm not suggesting that we can't work this out, but it seems to me that it might be much easier if we reached out to her teacher. After all, she seems to have quite a way with the children, especially Iowa…"

"My dear, I'm afraid you still don't understand me." Once again, he turned toward Mrs. Smith. "Iowa is our responsibility, and we need to handle the situation our way. I agree with you that Mrs. Royce has quite a way…"

"Ms. Royce, dear."

"Ms. Royce has a quite a way with children like Iowa, but we would be shirking our responsibility if we brought her in – and I am only speaking theoretically – if we brought her in now. We need some time to do this our way, just like we've done countless times before. Look," he added, and the expression on his face seemed to soften, "you're a remarkable woman yourself, and I'm confident that if anyone can get through to her, it's you."

Mrs. Smith reached up and kissed her husband slightly on the cheek. She nestled back down in his side, and practically purred. "Thank you, dear. But I am a little worried. The situation is different this time. Iowa is our child now, and I think we need to act more like parents than…well, do you understand what I'm getting at? I think it's just fine if we invite Ms. Royce over to help. And I don't think anyone would think the less of us if we did, because this is what parents do from time to time. We don't get to throw up our hands this time if things don't work out. Am I making sense?"

"You always make sense, my dear. But let's hold off for right now. If things change, then we'll do exactly what you suggest. Right now…right now, let's do things my way and we'll see what happens."

"All right, dear, as long as you remember that Iowa is not just a contract."

Mr. Smith smiled wanly, and turned his gaze back toward the opposite wall. "By the way, who are these idiot friends of hers?"

"I wonder if we should go out looking for her? I know you said it's pointless, but what if there's a chance that we…that we find her, that's all."

"No, it's a waste of time, and, besides, we need to be here in case she comes back. What if she calls and we aren't here?"

"Maybe you should go out, and I'll stay here."

Mr. Smith hesitated. He was genuinely concerned about Iowa. But at the same time, he was angry that she had disregarded the rules, even if he hadn't articulated them, and he didn't want her thinking that she could get away with such behavior – that she was calling the shots – which she might if he came looking for her, or if she came home, chatted with Mrs. Smith, and went to bed while he was out scouring the neighborhood for her. If only her mother had bequeathed Iowa to someone else, he considered with a slight shake of his head, then he could have resolved the situation in a flash and wouldn't have given a second thought about it. "Yes, perhaps you're right," Mr. Smith began slowly, almost indifferently, "but…but we have to show her that there are consequences for her actions – and especially so if she spoke to her mother before the end – and I don't think we can accomplish that if we allow her to run the show. She needs to learn a lesson that neither her father nor mother had the good sense to teach her. Plus, as I said before, if we force her to come back, if she doesn't come back on her own, she's going to do this again and again, and sooner or later we will arrive at a point in which we can no longer control her. Do you see the reason behind my actions?" He wasn't completely convinced, but he was confident that Mrs. Smith would be and would defer to him.

"Yes, I suppose," she replied. "I'm still worried, but nothing comforts me as much as sitting next to you, my dear."

"I feel the same way."

Chapter Twelve - Iowa's absence didn't attract a lot of attention

Iowa's absence at school didn't attract a lot of attention, except among the Cygnets. Since she didn't have many friends outside of the Cygnets, no one noticed or cared whether she was in school or not. Certainly, some of her teachers, especially Ms. Royce, conveyed their concern to school authorities, but the authorities like the police felt that they could only do so much for a runaway, and that much wasn't very much.

But Ms. Royce was concerned, deeply concerned. She had a strong inkling of what had happened, although at the moment she was powerless to do anything to help Iowa. She didn't know where the girl had gone, but she hoped that Iowa would reach out to her – and if she did that, Ms. Royce knew exactly what to do and how to help. She had seen the same thing happen before, and she was confident that she could be useful if she could intervene before things reached a state of no return – after that, only the most extreme measures could contain, but not eliminate, the problem. However, until Iowa reached out, Ms. Royce was helpless to do anything except wait and hope.

The Cygnets were as much in the dark as everyone else. Everyone was in touch almost every day, especially during school, and so they knew when someone was sick, overslept, or had simply skipped a class for whatever reason (which wasn't often). They knew so much about each other that had Iowa actually run away from home in the traditional sense, they would have known that it was going to happen practically the very second that Iowa or anyone else knew it. And not only this, they would have known where she went, where she was staying, her state of mind, and practically everything else. If she had wanted to come home, they would have known that, too, and would have been able to help her return. If she needed money, they would have been aware of that and would have done everything they could to get some money to her, even though money was a harder resource to come by than such simple necessities as food and clothing. In short, they would have been tracking Iowa's movements before, during, and after she left home, and they would have been in constant contact with the girl, even if it were only the occasional call from a gas station or roadside convenience stop.

However, Iowa's disappearance was a complete mystery to them. Not only had she left the lake without a word, but she had disappeared without giving anyone the slightest hint that she was considering such an action. The Cygnets knew that Iowa hated the Smiths and would not have gone anywhere with those horrible people if it meant losing touch with her real family – the Cygnets – and at the same time they also knew that she would not have kept anything from her friends. True, she hadn't said much about her father's death, but she didn't keep the fact from the Cygnets and, as they all were aware, something things are best left unsaid, or briefly said. They accepted this, just as they accepted Iowa's quirks and eccentricities, because that's how families are -- because that's how brothers and sisters are, if they love one another like the Cygnets loved each other – and so while Iowa's disappearance was strange and disturbing to the community, it was doubly so to the Cygnets, who needed to understand her behavior toward Luke and wanted to know why she could have disappeared without a single word of explanation. Naturally, all of this would have been forgotten had she been abducted, and yet it seemed fairly clear that nothing of the kind had happened, since there were no school notices regarding her disappearance, no fliers on buildings, utility poles, or milk cartons. Regardless, they didn't completely turn their backs on Iowa – they still hoped for an explanation that would make sense of her treatment of Luke and her disappearance – even though they felt powerless to do anything except wait and watch for signs that she was coming back or reaching out to them. It should not be forgotten that for a while the Cygnets hoped that Iowa would return to the lake (what better place to go to communicate with them?), and so each day one or more of them would venture to the lake, search the clearing and surrounding shore, scour the woods, either for Iowa herself or signs that she had been there. But because the result each day was disheartening, it was becoming harder and harder for the Cygnets to believe that Iowa had not severed her ties with the only true family she had ever had.

"She would have called or something," moaned Dana, as the three members of the Cygnets met in the cafeteria for lunch one day about three weeks after Iowa disappeared. This was not the first time the subject had come up, although the thrust of the conversations had always been the same. "Someone should do something. What is her mother...I mean, the Smiths doing? Aren't they worried?"

"If they're not worried, then something else much be going on," said Lu. "But I thought Iowa said she didn't trust them. She seemed to be afraid of them for some reason."

"No, Iowa said she didn't like them, and she might have to move out of town with them at the end of the school year," Press said calmly, reasonably.

"Isn't that what I said? She was afraid of them."

"No, I don't think she was afraid of them as much as she was afraid of leaving us. How would you feel if you had to leave?" Press felt that Lu was being stupid.

"Okay, then why didn't she tell anyone? She could have stayed with one of us for a while at least?"

"You have a point," Luke interjected. "But I wonder if something else was going on. She was behaving weirdly after her mother died. Maybe she just left to get away for a while and felt bad about telling us – or just didn't want to tell us. Sister or not, she can behave inconsistently sometimes."

"She was certainly being weird around you," Dana added. "You have a fight or something? What was the problem? If I didn't know better, I'd say you two didn't like each other."

"No, that isn't it. I still like her; nothing's changed. But she sometimes acted like she didn't like me. Or maybe something I did irritated her. I don't know. She never told me. When she was mean, it always seemed like it was up to me to find out why. But I asked, and she didn't say anything."

"Asked what?" Lu asked, and then promptly forgot her question.

"Yes, she was getting a little weird for a while," added Dana, after which she and the others fell silent. Lost in thought, none of them noticed that the cafeteria had emptied and that everyone had gone to their classes.

One of the cleaning ladies, an elderly woman with a big smile and even bigger glasses (the lenses of which made her eyes seem unusually large and blurry), interrupted their reverie by telling them that she had to close down and clean up. "Anyway, aren't you late for class?" she added for good measure. The four of them jumped up and headed for class, promising each other to meet at the lake on Friday, the day after tomorrow.

The Cygnets met, but to their disappointment Iowa was not there. Something about the conversation and the promise to meet filled them with an expectation that Iowa would be there, greeting them with smiles and hugs and promising never to disappear again. They had even expected her to be filled with great stories that would fire their imaginations for days, after which things would settle down and everything would again be as it once had been, before Iowa disappeared. But even though these expectations evaporated Friday evening, none of the Cygnets believed that they had seen the last of Iowa, even though during the weekend and throughout the following days and weeks, it was becoming increasingly difficult to envision a time when Iowa would return and things would indeed be as they once were.

After several months of visiting the lake and hoping that Iowa would be there, and after more than a few lunch and evening conversations speculating on her whereabouts, the Cygnets finally gave up on Iowa. It had become clear that she was not going to reach out to any of them, much less return to the lake and the arms of her closest friends. But even if she did return some Saturday evening, standing at the edge of the water, her arms open and her smile nearly as big as her face, none of the other Cygnets were certain that they could be as open and welcoming, unless perhaps she had the greatest excuse in the world for having been silent all this time. Not even Dana could come up with such a suitable excuse. In fact, Iowa's absence and her silence only magnified her faults -- which were easily overlooked prior to her disappearance – making her seem like someone who should never have been allowed to join the Cygnets. She was cranky, after all, and she had a vendetta against Luke, whom she had viciously attacked and then tried to blame for the violence. Who knows what she would have done to Lu had she been given half a chance? Luckily, as Lu herself recalled, Luke stood up for her and, braving Iowa's most contemptible behavior, kept Lu and everyone else safe from Iowa's malicious behavior. There were times, though, when they tried to understand why Iowa had struck Luke, but since he didn't know and his explanations were often unsatisfactory, they tended to believe that he was covering up something that reflected poorly on the girl. Luke was unfailingly kind, after all.

Six months had passed, and the Cygnets and everyone else seemed to have forgotten about Iowa. The Cygnets continued on – meeting at the lake and keeping to themselves during school lunch – and so did school and practically everything else that used to be associated with Iowa. Press heard that the Smiths had left town and that the house she had grown up in had been sold. It may have been the selling of the house that finally made the Cygnets cease talking about Iowa, as if the sale underlined the finality of her absence. Whatever happened to Iowa was no longer a concern. Besides, even if they wanted to do something, there was nothing they could do to bring back their former friend and repair all the damage that she had caused. Iowa was gone (probably living with the Smiths), and that was that.

Chapter Thirteen - One evening long after Iowa's absence

One evening long after Iowa's absence, Luke called the Cygnets and informed them that he had spoken to Iowa and that if they were interested, she would meet them at the lake Saturday afternoon, which was the following afternoon. Luke didn't have much more information beyond that, other than she sounded good and was quite pleasant. "Iowa told me she realized how badly she treated me, and she apologized, saying it would never happen again," he added. "But that's just about it. She said she didn't have much time to talk, but she hoped everyone could make it. She sent her love, too."

Everyone was surprised – no, everyone was shocked – but they weren't anxious to see her, for even though she apologized to Luke, there was still the past and her bright, happy tone (these were Luke's words) was offensive, given the circumstances, and "just like Iowa." In fact, from what they could gather from Luke, it sounded like she had no intention of telling them the truth and that she was counting on their love to gloss over minor things like facts and reality. What kind of friend—what kind of friend! – would act that way; you treat acquaintances that way, but not family, not the Cygnets. Still, each of them resolved to meet Iowa, and if they couldn't be as happy about her reappearance as Luke clearly was, then at least they could demand to know why she disappeared and why she hadn't informed them of her intentions. Press was perhaps the most offended, because in Iowa's absence she had become the de facto focal point around which the others gravitated, and she did not want to lose that position simply because Iowa returned, regardless of the circumstances before and after her disappearance. None of them, including Press, was heartless, and there was a place in each of them that remembered Iowa with fondness, even if they didn't know what to expect when and if they saw her again. Since they had not planned to meet before the big event, none of them aired their feelings or tried to understand how the others felt.

Saturday afternoon was warm and sunny, a perfect spring morning, with flowers in bloom – the colors (reds, blues, yellows, and whites, especially the whites -- small, white flowers were everywhere throughout the park) were amazing, and the scent filled one's nose and made one feel happy and optimistic. The Cygnets arrived at the entrance of the park at the same time, and, for a moment before entering, they looked at one another and then at the tall trees, which were all in bloom and so thick that in some places they prevented most of the light from reaching the ground. They were pleased to see one another, and without saying so they were thankful that everyone came out, because it almost seemed that they were going to encounter a momentous event or maybe even a strange apparition, and no one wanted to do that alone. Without a word, they walked single file into the park and, staying on the path, headed directly for the lake. Normally, they would have walked side-by-side, unconsciously taking turns leading the fifteen minute or so journey to the edge of the water. The path was certainly wide enough to accommodate all five Cygnets (when there were five), but this time they all fell in line behind Luke, because he was the one who had spoken to Iowa, he was the one who had insisted that they meet her at the lake, and by and large they were all engrossed (at least in the beginning) in their own thoughts on the matter. Halfway there, however, Press broke the silence.

"What else did Iowa say? Did she give you any clue why she wanted to see us now and not eons ago?" Press was genuinely curious, and at the same time she needed some justification for seeing someone who had abandoned the group, abandoned the very people she called her family.

"She didn't say anything else. Like I said, it was a short conversation, and we really only talked about meeting and explaining things."

"We certainly need an explanation," proffered Lu, without following up on the idea.

"I agree," Luke replied, and then added nothing else regarding this need.

"We need something," added Dana, "because she acted like she didn't need us..."

"Didn't want us," Press interjected.

"That's right, didn't want us and didn't need us."

"We don't need her, and maybe we don't want her either," mumbled Lu. "I'm not sure why we should be coming to her, as if we were at her beck and call."

Luke paused and turned to face the others. "You're all right, but I would like to see what she has to say. She owes us an explanation, and this is the time she can provide it. We don't have to change and welcome her back, but I think she has to explain things. Don't you?"

"I suppose. Maybe..."

"And, who knows, maybe she'll have a legitimate explanation..."

"Captured by gypsies, you mean, and unable to communicate with the outside world."

"No, I'm serious. I don't know what she'll have to say or whether what she does say will have any value to us, but I think we should give her a chance. We're a family, aren't we, and families at least listen? Right?"

"Maybe," said Press. "But are you sure she didn't say anything else, anything no matter how minor that might help us..."

"No, I told you everything. Look, if you don't want to go, that's fine. We're still family, and sometimes family can disagree and still be family. If you don't want to go, I can tell you later what she said. Okay?"

"No, we're all going," said Press, answering for everyone. "We just want to know what we're getting into by seeing her now. You understand that, right?"

Luke turned and continued walking. "Right," he said over his shoulder. Luke was as interested as the rest of them in what Iowa would say or do, although his interest in the girl seemed to be a little different, maybe even deeper. Even though it had been ages since he had seen her, he had never lost his interest in her or ceased to think about her from time to time. Perhaps it had something to do with the wound beneath his eye. The wound had healed nicely, but there was still a faint, barely perceptible mark that he couldn't help noticing every time he looked into the mirror. In fact, the wound had convinced him that there had been more to their interactions than had been apparent to him at the time. Now, instead of hating her for the mark beneath his eye, he liked her more because of it and felt that it was the visual representation (a seal or signature) of a bond or agreement between them. If this weren't the case, then why didn't she reach out to Press or one of the others instead of him? Why only him? She could have called every one of them, she could have apologized to each one individually, but instead she spoke only to him; she had made him the repository of her intentions. If this didn't mean something, then she was even stranger than anyone had thought.

The Cygnets arrived at the edge of the lake as planned, on time, but Iowa was nowhere in sight. Outside of the trees, the day seemed hot, just like summer, and the sun's bright glow was nearly as oppressive. Suddenly, a light breeze blew across the lake, covering its surface with small crests and cups, and forcing thin washes of water up on the smooth part of the shore. Even though the lake wasn't deep, the waves and its gray, sleet-like color made it look deep, almost like an ocean. The breeze also rustled the leaves on the trees, offering the only noise around them save for the occasional swish of water coming ashore. In the distance, hovering over the trees, a hawk lazily floated in the sky.

"Do you see her?" Press asked, looking around and peering into the woods.

"I don't see her," noted Lu with a slight pique in her voice. "She promised she would be here, and now she's nowhere to be seen."

"Hold on," Luke said trying to assuage the rising anger he sensed with the absence of Iowa. "She said she'll be here, and she'll be here. Look, if she doesn't come, then we'll stay and have a nice time by ourselves. We're not losing anything by coming here. We would have come here anyway, right?"

While Luke was trying to keep everyone calm, Press had been looking across the lake, observing its familiar shape, the trees dipping the tips of long branches into the water, and even the waves, which she had seen countless times before. She had begun to speculate on the kind of person who would toss all this away – the lake, the family, the Cygnets – when she noticed something in the water perhaps thirty feet offshore. Initially, it looked like an odd clump of debris (grass and cattails tangled around a bright piece of wood), but the more she stared at it, the more it began to resemble something familiar – maybe an animal – although it was still too far out to identify for certain. This bothered Press because it looked familiar and she couldn't identify it, and so she interrupted the increasingly acerbic conversation between Luke and the other Cygnets.

"Look," she said, pointing at the object. "What's that?"

All of them looked into the direct where Press was pointing, and all of them noticed the same clump of debris.

"What is it?" asked Lu.

"I don't know. Luke, can you see it clearly?"

The Cygnets as one body stared at the object, squinting and turning their heads this way and that. Lu broke the momentary silence. "I think those are clothes."

"I think someone's in the water, but they're not moving."

Luke, too, now saw clothing, but he also saw something else. In an instant, he thought he had recognized the now-bluish material floating in the waves – it looked like the blouse that Iowa often wore, or at least the color reminded him of such a blouse, the very one that she had worn on the last day he saw her, the day she nearly poked his eye out. Without further hesitation, Luke charged out into the lake toward the floating materials. Even though he was a strong swimmer, he didn't think once about swimming, because the water was no more than three, maybe four feet at that point.

And no sooner had he starting crashing through the water than the others followed suit. Loud explosions of water, sprays of white foam, sprang up around them as they moved toward the clothing, that they were all now certain was Iowa.

Luke was the first to reach the clothing. When he was about five feet away – when it was just out of reach of even his long arms -- it was clear that the clothing covered someone, and when he was next to it and reached down and pulled it fully to the surface, he could see that it was what he feared most in the world – the lifeless body, which he had trouble holding out of the water, was Iowa. There was no question. He recognized her face – it hadn't changed over the months – and as he held it in his arms, trying to keep his feet while at the same time holding the dearest face he had ever seen above the splashing waves, he recognized the very body, its curves and angles, that he had once longed to hold in a strange, natural embrace. Once the others arrived, they too recognized Iowa, and it was at that moment that Luke, still holding the motionless body of their sister, slipped onto the seat of his pants while still keeping Iowa's face out of the water.

"Oh, God," cried Lu, "It's Iowa." Standing three feet from Luke and the lifeless Iowa, she broke down in tears and was practically inconsolable. Press, realizing that nothing could help Iowa now, went over to Lu and, holding her in her arms, tried to calm her down. Dana, however, stepped closer and looked at Iowa in the face. "If she's dead," she said, "It didn't happen very long ago. She seems to have good color…Luke, I'm not sure she's dead. Let's bring her to shore."

Luke responded immediately without question and, jumping up, he pulled and carried Iowa to shore, where he carefully laid her down on a clearing just beyond the lip of the water. Neither he nor the others, except Press, knew what to do at that point. But just as Press got down on her knees to check for Iowa's breathing, Iowa sat up and, barely containing her laughter, warned Press not to "do any of that mouth-to-mouth stuff."

Chapter Fourteen - The Cygnets stood back

The Cygnets stood back and stared down at Iowa, who continued to laugh. Once she began to settle down, she kept saying, "If you could have seen your faces," after which she crumpled over in another spasm of laughter. This went on for perhaps a good two or three minutes more before she had regained enough composure to sit up and look every one of the Cygnets in the face. And they looked at her, dourly examining the person they had tried to forget, who had treated them so shabbily, and who now was making fun of them. It was all a big joke, and it was lucky that Luke was just as horrified as the rest, for if he had shown the least bit of appreciation for her joke, the Cygnets would have thought him in cahoots with Iowa and would probably have cast him out of the group.

Luke was the first to speak. He was, after all, the person who had exposed them to this horrible prank. "I don't understand. What's this all about?"

"Do you think it's funny?" Press interjected, glowering at Iowa. "Do you think any of it's funny? We were worried about you when you disappeared, and now you return to play this horrible joke on us… treat us like garbage…and why is that funny? What kind of person are you?" Press's anger grew as she asked her questions, because in her mind she knew the answers. "Only a monster would behave this way, not a family member, not someone... You know, we can go anywhere to be treated this way, but we aren't going to let you treat us this way here, of all places." By the time she had finished, practically breathless, her anger had risen to such a pitch that she wanted to hit Iowa, to avenge Luke's injuries and those of the other Cygnets. Taking one step forward to do just that, she was stopped when Luke intervened.

"No, don't lower yourself," he said quietly, after which he stepped back and glowered at Iowa.

"Come on, it was only a joke," Iowa said, the smile on her face gone. In fact, the bright, impish expression on her face immediately after the joke had been replaced by an almost frightened seriousness that reflected the sincerity of her words and her understanding of the problem she had caused. "We've played jokes on one another before."

No one responded. Everyone looked at Iowa for a brief moment and then turned to leave, even Luke. "We'll need to find another place to hang out," Press informed the others as they began walking away.

"Stop...please. I'm sorry, I didn't mean to hurt anyone," Iowa called out, genuinely remorseful for her bad game. "Look, I felt bad for having been away for so long, and I only wanted you to laugh and not be angry. I was wrong. Please come back."

Luke, who had been leading the group, slowed and then stopped. Although he was put off by Iowa's joke, and, at the same time, felt that he should be the first person to leave since he had encouraged the others to speak to Iowa, he truly didn't want to go and was willing to consider almost any excuse to stay for a few more minutes. He turned and looked back at Iowa, who had risen and was now standing in her wet clothes looking at him and the others. "We're not going to play your games, Iowa."

"And I'm not going to play them anymore. Give me a chance to explain things. I promise you it will be worth your while. Please, give me one last chance."

Press was about to begin walking again, but she and the others stopped when Luke addressed Iowa in what was for him a firm, no-nonsense manner. "All right, Iowa, one last chance. But if you play one more of your stupid games, we're gone and not coming back." Press wasn't eager to go back, but since everyone else turned and was walking toward Iowa, she felt that she, too, had to give the girl the chance she begged for. 'Who knows,' she told herself. 'It might just be stupid enough that we can give up on her altogether.'

No one sat down. They all stood around Iowa as she began to explain the reason for her absence. She began with her mother's death, telling them how strange and cold she had felt immediately afterward, and then she explained the presence of the Smiths and highlighted the contempt that she felt toward them. She never liked them, and although they may have had their good sides, she wasn't about to let them take her away from school, the neighborhood, and, most importantly, the Cygnets -- quite likely forever.

"But you left us anyway," Press added.

"But I came back. Look, my life was ending at that moment, and I couldn't think straight. I was desperate to do something, and I didn't know where to turn. I..."

"You could have turned to us," Dana added.

"Yes, you're right. And I would have, except for one thing that my mother told me just before she passed away – and that one thing changed my life so profoundly that I...well, the time went by so quickly, and I finally had the peace and security I craved, that...that I don't know what happened. All I know is that it happened so quickly it seems like yesterday I hit Luke. And Luke, I can't begin to tell you how sorry I am."

"So what was the one thing that was so important?" Press challenged her.

"I'm going to tell you, and you'll understand why it is so important and why I couldn't tell you before. My mother told me never to tell a soul, unless that soul is worthy and trustworthy. I promised her I wouldn't, and I was prepared to keep the secret to myself for as long as I lived until...until I realized that I could tell you; I could tell all of you. Really, I need to tell you, and I know that no one is more worthy of this secret than you – all of you – and I'm sorry that it took me so long to realize it."

"You didn't know that before? And now all of a sudden you have this big secret?" Press wasn't ready to accept her story, especially because she wasn't ready to accept her back in the Cygnets regardless of the conditions.

"Yes, but it isn't as simple as that. Look, I was confused, and what my mother told me was even more confusing. But when I followed her directions, when I lived the way I did…well, you have to believe me when I tell you that I'm sorry and that I want to make amends for what I did. And I will, if you listen to me for a few minutes." Iowa looked directly at everyone to demonstrate her sincerity, although at the same time she scanned their expressions for signs that they still didn't believe her or didn't care what she had to say. Press clearly wasn't moved. Some of the others were, though, more or less, except Luke. She could see that Luke was giving her a second chance and, for the first time in years, she felt especially close to him.

"All right, what's the secret?"

Iowa was about to tell them, and then she thought better of this idea, since no one (especially Press) would believe it, and if they didn't immediately understand what she was telling them, they would probably leave, destroying any chance she had of explaining it to them and of reconciling with them. This is not to say that she had misgivings about telling and showing them; she did, but at the same time she felt that it was more important to let them in on her secret, to give them the same opportunity her mother gave her, and then let them decide for themselves what was right for them. It was a difficult decision either way, but in the end she felt that this was the correct one, even though four additional people would know.

She hesitated. "All right," she began. "Let me show you something first, and then we can discuss it." She turned and walked back into the water, about ten feet from the shore.

"Are you going to play dead again?" Press demanded.

"No, look carefully." Iowa faced them and, closing her eyes, lowering her chin, and pulling her arms close to her body, remained perfectly still. Everyone watched, wondering if she was going to pull another one of her bad jokes, when something strange began to happen. Initially, it was difficult to say what was happening, if indeed something was happening (there was), but as they watched Iowa they noticed that her skin and hair started to become lighter, as if a bright light were shining on her and bleaching away all her color. Iowa always had fair skin and hair, but under the imaginary light, she was becoming fairer and actually turning white, a white that seemed almost inhuman. But if this weren't enough, other strange changes began to take place, and taking place one after another with incredible speed, as if time was speeding up the transformation of the girl, and within seconds her clothes – the plain blue blouse and jeans – began to lose their color as well, the various blues fading and either becoming translucent or as white as Iowa's skin, for they became indistinguishable from the rest of Iowa – they were no longer clothes but Iowa herself, or what seemed to be Iowa.

Wide eyed and open mouthed, the Cygnets stared as Iowa's changes continued, but now the changes were starting to become more radical than merely changing the color of one's face, hair, and clothing -- her body began to push and pull itself, as if there was some strange and violent force inside her stretching her neck, distending her stomach, and shrinking her legs (she almost seemed to be sinking in the lake). Her neck, which was now hardly more than a couple of inches in diameter, began to stretch upward until it reached a grotesque, undulating length, while her head correspondingly shrank until it was no bigger than Luke's fist – a fist with two black eyes that seemed to be observing the Cygnets as they observed it. Iowa's shoulders quickly disappeared, her arms flattened against the sides of her body, making them almost indistinguishable with her body, and then her body began contracting and elongating so that her stomach was round and her back arched and flattened at its end. Iowa's legs, seeming to starve and shrivel up until they were little more than a couple of ungainly sticks, cast off their white hue and turned a peculiar yellowish orange; shortly after this, her entire body (except her legs) seemed to be getting softer, less defined, and she appeared to be covered with something that resembled the soft down of baby chicks. Slipping beneath the surface of the water as if it were the most natural thing to do, Iowa, or whatever she had become, disappeared from sight, leaving in her wake a single, barely perceptible ripple.

None of the Cygnets knew what to make of this, although a couple of them began to wonder if she was up to her old practical jokes again and would surface laughing at them the very second they expressed their concern. But as the seconds ticked off and Iowa failed to breach the surface, each one of them became concerned and, as if by silent agreement, they slowly began walking toward the water's edge to get a better view and, if need be, wade out to the spot where she had been standing. If she were hurt, if she had somehow got tangled up in the rocks and weeds under the water and couldn't surface, they would never have forgiven themselves for having dismissed the obvious signs of danger. But before they reached the water, a white swan breached the surface and began swimming toward them.

Chapter Fifteen - The Cygnets were dumbfounded

The Cygnets were dumbfounded. Lu shrieked and hid her eyes, Press and Dana stood with open mouths, and Luke fell back on the seat of his pants. The swan swam toward them until it could swim no longer and then with heavy, ungainly steps, it walked out of the water and over to Luke, where it stopped, honked, and then settled down on the ground next to him, leaning against his leg. None of them, not even Luke ventured to touch the bird, and when it was clear that the animal was not going to bite anyone, they began asking themselves what had happened and whether Iowa was still in the water, perhaps holding her breath while they puzzled over a swan that just happened to swim by.

"Maybe she tied it down and released it when she went under," Press suggested, not willing to accept the obvious just yet.

"No way," Luke responded, sliding away from the bird and standing up, after which he stepped away from the animal. "You can't keep it under water for that length of time without killing it."

"So what happened?" asked Dana. "What did we see?"

"Take it away. I don't want to see it," Lu continued moaning. "Let's leave."

"My God, I can't believe it. What happened to her?" someone else said, although no one looked at the speaker, whoever it was.

"What happened to Iowa? Where is she?"

Suddenly, the swan got up and slowly waddled from one person to the other, looking at each one in the face. When apparently satisfied, it turned and walked away from the others and, after glancing at each one of them more time, it found a spot on the ground to nestle down, after which it rolled to its side. As they stood watching it – and they couldn't do anything but stand and watch the animal – it began to twist and turn, as if it were dying and struggling to get up and to return to a place of safety.

"It's dying," Lu pleaded, "Shouldn't we do something?"

Before they had a chance to do anything, the animal began to assume monstrous proportions – its head and neck were inflating and its legs were stretching outward. No one said anything, not even Lu, as it continued writhing, changing shape, and finally gaining color – its formerly white feathers were gone and in their place were Iowa's blue blouse and jeans, which neatly fit the prostrate girl, who was motionless.

Running over to her, they stopped as she stood up and slowly brushed off the dirt from her clothes. She looked at them coolly, as if she couldn't quite recognize them, and then as the brightness came back into her dark eyes, she said, "Do you understand now?"

"Is that a trick? How did you do it?" demanded Press.

"It's not a trick," Iowa responded.

"Well, you don't just look like a swan without doing some sort of trick."

"I didn't just look like a swan. I was a swan. I was a real swan. Everything you saw was real – my body was real, and my mind…it was a swan's mind. I can't explain that very well, but I had all the sensations and perceptions that swans have, and maybe a little more. There was still part of my mind that was human, but all the rest…all the rest was a swan. Didn't you see? I can think like a swan, swim like a swan, and I suppose fly like a swan. I don't know if swans can fly. I don't think so, but I've never tried. Do you understand?"

"I can't believe it. People don't turn into swans. Have you become a magician, Iowa?" Press insisted.

"No, we saw what we saw," Luke added calmly and forcefully. "I believe her. I saw it with my own eyes."

"You're in on it with her. You were in on it from the start. You were the one she contacted, you were the one who led us here, and now you are the one who is helping her pull one of her bad games."

"It's not true…," Luke began to say, but Press interrupted him.

"That's what you say. What I say is we leave here and leave those two lovebirds to their filthy tricks." Press turned to go, but Iowa grasped her arm to stop her. Press turned quickly, twisting out of Iowa's grip and grabbing Iowa's arm, tightly.

"Don't ever touch me again, Iowa. Do you understand me?" Press stared at her briefly, and then released her, pushing her arm away.

Iowa stepped away from Press. "I won't," she said, glancing at the others before turning back to Press. "It's not a trick, and Luke isn't in on anything."

"Then why did you call him first? Why didn't you call the rest of us? And why did you play that stupid drowning game?"

"I called Luke, because I knew he'd listen to me. I called him, because I could count on him to tell everyone. I called Luke, because I knew you would react just the way you're reacting now, and I needed to get everyone here so I could talk to you all, explain it to you. Listen," Iowa pleaded and, turning away from Press, looked into the faces of each of the Cygnets, "I am not playing a game. I'm sorry for the drowning routine. I don't know how many times I can say it, but I'm sorry. I'm sorry. I'm sorry! I wanted…it doesn't matter. I wanted to come back to show you this and give you the same chance that I had. Listen: do you know where I was? I didn't run away, I was here, in this lake, swimming here day after day, living as a swan. Please listen. I know this sounds farfetched, but it was real. You saw the change a few minutes ago. If you thought I was faking it, then why didn't you touch me or do something to expose me? Luke, I was leaning against your body – did I feel like a fake? Did I look like a fake? If nothing else, how did I get so small? Luke, you saw me – is it possible for any human being to look like that? And all of you must have seen me over there" – she pointed to the clearing behind her – "change back. What did you see? If you don't think it was real, then prove it. Prove it!"

"I don't know what I saw," Dana said quietly. "But, I say, can you do it again?"

"Yes, I can do it again. I can do it a thousand times. And I can be a swan as long as I want, until I die, if I want."

"Can you show us how to do it?"

"Yes, yes, that's why I came back, to show you how to do it. It's a miraculous gift, and it's not fake, and no one else can do it without first being shown where the power to do it comes from. That's what's strange and miraculous. We all have the power to do it, but no one except me knows how. No one. I know only because my mother showed me. My father knew how to do it, too. Maybe there are others, but I don't know who they are, and it really doesn't matter. All that matters is that I can show you how to change your lives anytime you want. It's no trick. It's not fake. Do you want to know why I didn't say anything until now?"

Only Luke muttered "yes."

"It's because I hated my life. You have no idea what was happening. But once I turned into a swan – or once I realized that I could become a swan – I left all that behind and…and became a swan. I lived, breathed, and ate like a swan, and the only concerns I had were a swan's concerns. I was able to escape everything, my life, the Smiths, everything. Do you know where I was? I was here, at the lake, all this time. I never once left. I saw you every time you were here. I saw you sitting around and talking about me, wondering what happened. I saw it all. I heard it all. I was right over there when you were here." Without turning around, Iowa gestured with her thumb to the trees and shadows on the opposite side of the lake.

"I saw everyone one of you. But...but I didn't tell you, I didn't show myself, because I was living a life like no other in this world. I don't know how else to explain it – I was living a life so extraordinary that I didn't want to leave it and come back to face the Smiths and all the rest, not even for a few seconds. I don't know how else to explain it, but you'll understand if you listen to me. Yes, I wanted to see you, but...well, it wasn't until I truly understood that I could share this power with you that I felt compelled to come back. Do you understand? I am willing to risk everything to give you this power. If you don't want to learn it, that's okay. If you decided that you want me to leave permanently, that's okay, too, although I will always love you. But if you want me to show you – show you and no one else in the world – show you the most miraculous power in the world, then stay and listen to me. Let me show you." Iowa looked at each of the Cygnets, defying them to take their eyes off of her.

"You'll show us, and we can become swans too?"

"Yes, you can become a swan, too, just like I did. But the amazing thing is that you don't have to become a swan. You can become any animal you want."

"Any animal?"

"Yes, it's extraordinary. But I have to warn you – once you become an animal, you can only be that animal. You won't be able to turn into any other kind of animal. Once a swan, always a swan…or a human. You can change back like I did. But I can't be anything but a swan. Maybe there's a way of doing it, but I don't know how to do it. But yes, it was my intention to show you how to do it."

Everyone, including Press, was now willing to give Iowa the time she needed. Sitting on the logs and clumps of grass that they always sat on, the Cygnets listened as Iowa explained how to choose an animal, the limitations of being an animal, and what to do when you don't want to be an animal any more or when you need a break and want human company. She also stressed that when being an animal, one had to be careful and not overdo it, because there could come a time when the power to change back could be forgotten or out of one's control, which happened to her father. She told them many other things besides, until one by one she showed them how to make the change. She began with Press, then Lu and Dana, and last of all Luke. Luke was last not for any special reason. He had trouble thinking of the right animal and wanted to see what happened to the others before making his choice.

Chapter Sixteen - Iowa expected Press to make the change quickly

Iowa expected Press to make the change quickly and easily. She was certainly motivated – she was the first to volunteer – and, since she was in great physical shape, Iowa had little reason to doubt that she could handle the strains and stresses on the body that changing exacted. Naturally, anyone can make the change, even Dana, and yet there are often moments during the process that are so tiring (your muscles ache and your eyes burn) that it is easy to doubt the value of returning to human form. Iowa couldn't help recalling the first time she had gone completely through the process. After changing back to a human, she went to her room in the middle of the day and slept for fifteen hours straight.

Once Press stepped forward, Iowa detailed the process and reiterated the irrevocability of her choice, which Press took in with a seriousness that surprised Iowa. She had never seen Press so intent upon anything before, unless it was a game or contest of some kind. Iowa was even more surprised that after all her warnings and the animosity that Press had shown her only a few minutes ago, Press chose to become a swan. Congratulating her on the choice, Iowa was careful not to make too much of it, because she didn't want Press to change her mind or become wishy-washy about her choice – one had to choose and keep to that choice –

especially since she was pleased, because it meant that she would have someone to keep her company on the lake and that whatever ill-will Press had against her was now gone, or nearly so. At any rate, having all the instruction and advice that she would ever need, Iowa stood back and let Press go to work.

Press smiled at Iowa and, turning around, smiled at each of the others. There was something in her smile – a sad twist at the corner of her lips, perhaps, or the unusual amount of moisture in her eyes – that made them all think that she was going on a long journey and might not see them again in the foreseeable future, which of course none of them truly believed. Turning back to Iowa, Press seemed to have regained her composure and, without another word, she closed her eyes, lowered her head, and, after taking several deep breaths (evidently the air calmed her nerves and gave her the energy Press knew she would need to change successfully), held her arms around her body and began the process of turning into a swan in front of everyone. There would be no denying it if anyone still harbored doubts. The seconds ticked off and then a minute, and another minute, and then nothing. Press stayed as she was. Undeterred – clearly, she wasn't concentrating enough – she opened her eyes, smiled again at Iowa, adjusted her stance (increasing the distance between her feet, as though that would give her the added strength she needed to become a swan), and began again…with the same result as before. A quick smile to Iowa (she didn't glance at the others, possibly because she didn't want to reveal her confusion), several more deep breaths – deeper than any past breaths, as if the lack of sufficient oxygen might be playing a role in failure to change – and tried it again, and again the result was the same. Press didn't have a feather on her, and her skin was as tanned as it ever was.

Initially, Press was embarrassed, because she attributed her failure to change to some kind of personal failure, letting down both Iowa and the Cygnets. Hanging her head, she apologized to Iowa and, without turning toward them, the Cygnets. Iowa had begun to reassure her that no apologies were warranted, because the first change was the most difficult and often required several tries before achieving a successful change. After that, it was a piece of cake, and Press should be able to go back and forth – human to swan and back again – at will, and within seconds. But just as Iowa began to relate all the difficulties she had had with her change – including her doubts regarding the accuracy of her mother's instructions and her, Iowa's, own ability to make the change – Press started to suspect that it was all a hoax and that Iowa was making fun of her, trying to get back at Press for standing up to her and calling her out because of her ill treatment of the Cygnets. Press might have taken a step back and laughed at Iowa, pretending that she had been pretending and that she didn't for a moment believe that anyone could change into an animal (naturally, she would have been at a loss to explain Iowa's transformation, but could have dismissed it as a joke without explaining how it was performed, which should have been obvious, she would have added), but Iowa, sensing her consternation, stepped next to Press and whispered in her ear to relax and it will happen, and that was enough to calm Press's nerves and push her to try again, and again, if need be.

"Take your time," Iowa whispered, sounding like a knowledgeable adult, as she stepped back.

Press did as she was told and, for a few more seconds, it appeared that she would again fail. But after a minute of intense, motionless concentration during which everyone held their breath, something began to happen -- Press began to grow indistinct, white, elongated, and strangely deformed. A few seconds after this, she had become a swan. Honking and shaking her tail, she waddled into the water and began swimming parallel to the shore and then out toward the center of the lake.

Everyone watched. No one could take their eyes off Press. And as she swam gracefully back to the shore, back to where the Cygnets were standing, Iowa wondered if Press was going to have difficulty changing back to human form – if, indeed, she wanted to change back – since she had had so much difficulty in her initial change, far more than Iowa herself had experienced. Luckily, Iowa's fears were misplaced, for as soon as Press reached the shore, she waddled over to the very spot where Iowa had changed back and began her own reverse change. Everyone was mesmerized, and none more so than Press, who immediately after assuming human form, began chattering away about what she felt and how easy the change was.

"You won't believe it, you won't believe it," she practically screamed for the twentieth time. "I was swimming, and you won't believe it but I thought of almost nothing but being a swan. I don't know how to explain it. The only thing I can say is that everything felt completely natural – it was as if I had known how to paddle and flap my arms all my life – and what's more, I not only felt like a swan, but I thought like one, too. No, I didn't forget any of you. I just looked at everyone through the eyes of a swan, and my main concern was not to show off to everyone, but simply to soak up the sun, think about food, and…and I don't know what else. Can you believe it? Can you believe it? I thought like a swan. I never experienced anything like it. I had human thoughts, too, I suppose, because otherwise I wouldn't have come back. But they didn't seem to be…I don't know, I knew I had to come back, but I also knew that I could return any time I wanted. That's right, isn't it Iowa, I can change at will? You did say that, didn't you?"

Iowa smiled at her enthusiasm and remembered her own initial change. She had similar thoughts and feelings, although she didn't have anyone to share them with. "Yes, it's true. The next time it will be easier. But remember what I said. You have to be careful and not get too involved with the animal part of your nature, because it may be difficult to come back. Remember what I said about my father. My mother was much wiser, because she remembered the dangers and refused to get caught up in all that…whatever. Oh, and one more thing. Maybe the most important thing -- while you're a swan, you're not a human being.

You're a swan, and while you have all the advantages of a swan – or whatever animal you are – you have all its vulnerabilities as well. Don't try to act like a human without first changing back."

Everyone was crowded around Press, and she went on about her adventures – she went on far longer than she had been a swan -- often gesturing wildly (usually flapping her arms or craning her neck) to illustrate some point or other. But when the initial excitement began to wear thin, Lu insisted on taking a turn – and, no less surprising than in Press's case, she, too, wanted to be a swan. Iowa began with the same instructions, but while she prepared Lu, Press changed back into a swan and began swimming out on the lake. Lu's change, unlike Press's, was quick and simple, and in no time she was swimming on the lake. In fact, she immediately swam over to Press, and the two of them began frolicking as only swans can frolic, as if this was the first time they had set eyes on one another in years. Iowa was pleased, but she hoped they wouldn't overdo it, not on the first day. She didn't know if it was possible to overdo anything on the first day, but since there were many things she didn't know about the process of changing, she felt that initial moderation was probably best.

Dana was next and, by this time, it was no surprise that she wanted to be a swan. Dana was the easiest of all, contrary to what Iowa had expected. Dana wasn't strong and was always questioning things – not because she disagreed, but because she was naturally skeptical – but with her, everything went quickly and smoothly. Within minutes, all three were acting like long-lost friends, bouncing their long necks against one another and flapping their wings whenever one of them got too close. After a few minutes, they had all gone out to the farthest reaches of the lake and were rapidly swimming – to the degree that a swan can rapidly swim – from one end to the other.

While they were all engaged, and looked to be engaged for some time, Iowa turned to Luke and, smiling, asked him what he wanted to be. Unlike the others, Luke didn't have any idea what he wanted to be, not at that moment, anyway. He was certain, though, that he didn't want to be a swan, unless that was the only animal available to him. He couldn't explain it, but he didn't think he would fit in with the other swans. He had always fit in with the other Cygnets – "Just like one of the girls," Jimmy derisively said recently – but over the past year or so, he had begun to feel somewhat different, and the girls had begun to look at him differently, even though each one would have denied it had they been asked. Iowa's violent reaction to him last year was only an obvious manifestation of this change, but he knew that changes were brewing in the others as well, and he couldn't help wondering if the dynamics between them would ultimately be changed. Furthermore, Jimmy's mean comment changed something inside him as well. He was not a girl; he didn't want anyone to think of him as a girl; and so it occurred to him that the only way of keeping his sense of self while retaining his membership in the Cygnets was to become something else, something both he and the others would love and appreciate. Unfortunately, he couldn't quite figure out what it was, especially not then, especially not while Iowa was eyeing him and waiting for an answer.

"I don't know," he replied sheepishly. "I know you all want to be swans, but I'm not sure it's right for me. Is that okay? Do I have time to think?"

"Of course," Iowa replied with a friendly smile. She sensed his indecision, but she couldn't guess why he was undecided or why he wouldn't want to be a swan, especially since the others had no hesitation about the choice. "There's plenty of time. You don't have to decide now or even today. You can decide tomorrow, or the next day, or even next year. You've seen how it's done, and the timing and location are completely up to you."

"But what if I need help?" he asked, genuinely concerned. He wanted to become an animal, and at the same time he feared losing contact with Iowa, which he felt might somehow negatively affect his ability to change.

"No problem," she replied. "I will be here whenever you need help. I've decided to stay here at least until I'm twenty-one and the Smiths can't touch me."

Smiling, Iowa stepped back and within seconds had become a swan. She eyed Luke for a moment, twisting her head from one side to another almost like a dog, and then turned and, waddling over to the water and shaking her tail, stepped in and swam out to the others.

Luke sat down on a log about ten feet from the water's edge and watched the animals flapping their wings and swirling around one another; straining their long necks upward and intertwining them as if they were braiding a thick, feather-covered rope; and then after they had engaged in other similarly intimate activities, dipping their heads and necks beneath the water's surface and flipping water down their backs. Luke would have given just about anything to have joined them, but at the moment he just couldn't bring himself to change into a swan – he just didn't want to be a swan. Besides, he was beginning to suspect that even if he did become a swan, he couldn't join the others now as he had joined them a year ago when they were playing sticks. Something was indeed changing, and he had a sneaking suspicion that turning into a swan would do little if anything to arrest this change.

Sometime later, when everyone except Iowa felt that it was time to return home, they all swam to shore and returned to their human selves. Even Iowa changed, although only to say goodbye and ask them to hurry back. After the others eagerly agreed and disappeared into the trees on their way home, Iowa noticed that Luke was no longer in sight.

Chapter Seventeen - Everyone except Iowa met outside for lunch

The following day at school everyone except Iowa met outside for lunch. A warm breeze blew an occasional leaf between the tables, although neither the Cygnets nor anyone else appeared to notice. Normally, the Cygnets would be chattering away about this and that, but this day Press, Lu, and Dana spoke incessantly about what had happened yesterday at the lake.

"I couldn't believe it," Press kept saying. "It was the most wonderful sensation I've ever experienced. When I went home, my parents kept asking me if something was the matter and if something had happened. Can you believe it? For once I am totally happy, and they are worried that something is wrong, or that I have done something bad."

"My parents were angry I was out so late," Lu chimed in. "But I don't listen to them, and so it doesn't matter."

"It's still hard to believe it happened. Do you know what I did last night after everyone was asleep? I locked myself in the bathroom, filled the tub full of water, and changed right there. My mother must have heard me splashing around, and when she knocked on the door to ask what was going on, I had to turn back. But I did it, and it only took a couple of seconds, not like the first time. Did anyone else do it again?" Press, a slight smile on her lips, looked at each of them in turn, and when no one responded they all burst out laughing.

Luke, who did his best to smile when they smiled and laugh when they laughed, was pretty much ignored until Dana, just before they all got up to go to class, asked him why he didn't change. "Don't you want to?"

"Yes, very much," he replied, smiling at each of them. "But I don't know what to change to," he added, shrugging his shoulders. He had hoped his reply would be met with smiles, but everyone just stared at him, as if there was something wrong or aberrant with his answer.

"Why didn't you become a swan like the rest of us?" Lu asked, but the tone of her question seemed a little too harsh to Luke, as if he was the one who was refusing to join them and not the other way around.

"I don't know. I guess I didn't want to become a swan. It's not that I don't like them. I just don't want to be one."

"Then what do you want to be?"

"I haven't decided." No one responded to this. Instead, they all got up as if on cue and, continuing their conversation about what had happened, began walking to their classes. No one, however, insisted that Luke join them as they would have done in the past, and so Luke remained at the table for a few more minutes, finishing his milk and staring ahead at nothing in particular.

Jimmy came over and elbowed Luke in the shoulder. He was a head taller than Luke and looked several years older, although he was the same age. Luke never really liked Jimmy, because he often said mean things or taunted others for reasons known only to him, and the last thing he wanted to do now was to talk or listen to anyone, especially Jimmy. "Lose your girlfriends?" Jimmy asked, nudging him again. Luke refused to respond and got up and went to class.

That evening, Luke sat on the edge of his bed and mulled over the decision he would have to make. Everyone else in his house had been asleep for hours, and in fact Luke himself had been asleep for some time when something in the back of his mind forced him awake. Pulling off the covers and shifting his feet over the side of the bed, he sat up and tried to understand what he wanted and what the others wanted from him. He was certain that he didn't want to become a swan – he had nothing against the animals, despite the Cygnet name; they simply didn't appeal to his imagination – and yet something told him that if he didn't choose to be a swan, there would be negative consequences of one kind or another for him. It was troubling to think that there could be negative consequences of any kind with his choice, especially when there was practically an endless variety of choices he could make – he could be any animal he wanted to be, or else remain a human being and savor the possibility that he could make a choice in a heartbeat if he wanted to – and the very endlessness of his choices or possibilities was both exciting and alluring; and yet it was like owning a winning lottery ticket and being afraid to cash it because of all the taxes that would suddenly be due.

Luke wanted someone to help him make a decision, but the only person who could do that was Iowa, and to get her input now would require trudging out to the lake and searching for her in complete darkness, which had limited appeal because it was almost impossible to find her during the day. Clearly, he couldn't count on the Cygnets, even if he could reach them at this hour. They would chatter on about how great it was to be a swan, after which they would question his desire to be anything else, as if to be something else meant to be something other than a Cygnet. In fact, as he considered the Cygnet's possible reactions to his choice, Luke was beginning to suspect that being anything but a swan would be perceived as a rejection of the Cygnets, since they had clearly decided that a Cygnet could only be a swan. Naturally, none of them said as much, but it was obvious by the way they ignored him during lunch when he couldn't share their experiences at the lake, when he had nothing to offer about stretching necks, flapping wings, or shaking tails – and they had nothing to say about the fact that he was there, at the edge of the water, watching them while they gamboled about as if he weren't alive.

Luke closed his eyes and tried to clear his mind. 'But why not become a swan?' he asked himself. Did it really matter so much what he became, if becoming a swan meant that he retained his friendships with the Cygnets and maybe became a little closer to Iowa? Did it really matter so much and, if not, was he truly willing to risk it all for nothing, for the sake of becoming one animal as opposed to another? Who cares what animal you become as long as your friendships – your family – remain intact? Opening his eyes, Luke stared into the darkness surrounding him and listened, once again, to the intense silence, which was broken only now and then by the creaks and groans of the old house he lived in.

Breathing deeply, he told himself again that it didn't matter, that he could be any animal as long as he was happy, and yet as he tried to imagine changing into a swan and swimming around the lake with the Cygnets, something deep in the darkness whispered to him that he was being foolish. Indeed, he could become a swan, and for a while he could swim and play with the others just as he always did, paddling from one end of the lake to the others and back again, going as many times and as fast as the others wanted until they were all exhausted and waddled out of the water and relaxed on the shore, in the very clearing that had been their special place for as long as they had been Cygnets. But maybe it would only be for a while, because the more he tried to visualize their time together, the more he began to realize that these times would be short-lived; they wouldn't last forever. Sooner or later they would have to end – he felt it just as surely as anything else, even if he didn't exactly understand why – and, besides that, it was hard even under the best of circumstances to imagine them allowing him to wrap his neck around theirs, or scoop up water in his mouth and allow it to dribble down their backs. Yes, it might happen for a short time, but sooner or later they would put a stop to it either by ignoring him or indulging in such games by themselves without inviting him.

"No," he whispered to himself, needing to break the oppressive silence that was encouraging him to consider things he would never have considered during a bright, noisy day. "No, they're not like that. They would never do that," he added, watching dark shadows dance around his room. Closing and opening his eyes and shaking his head, Luke refused to consider any circumstances in which the Cygnets would turn against him simply because of the minor differences between him and the others. "No, no, no," he reiterated, as if he was chanting some magic charm that would ward off bad thoughts and keep his friendships intact. He had always known there were differences, but since these differences had never mattered before, there was absolutely no reason to suspect that these would matter now, especially since he was still the same person he had been the very first day he had met them (he couldn't remember which one he met first) and, if he had to, he would become a swan. "It would be fun being a swan," he added in a normal voice, speaking calmly and clearly to demonstrate his rationality and to cast aside thoughts and suppositions that were nothing more than the stuff of fantasy. "And they haven't changed a bit. We will always be the best of friends, no matter what." Having said this, he shook his head and dropped his chin to his chest.

No, he told himself, he had blown everything out of proportion, basing his fears on…on what? On the fact that they ignored him, or acted as if he was letting them down by not becoming a swan? No, it was ridiculous, although it was true that they had eyed him rather coldly – looking at him as if he had rebuffed their friendship – when he refused to commit himself to becoming a swan; and it was also true that they had left him at the lunch table without saying a single word to him. Luke couldn't imagine a single one of them speaking to him at this moment unless he committed to becoming a swan, maybe unless he could prove that he had made the change. But why bother? If they were going to act that way, then there was no point in becoming one of those stupid birds; and if this was what was required – to become a bird and do everything they tell him to do – then maybe he no longer wanted to be a member of the Cygnets. If they couldn't accept his choice – just as they all accepted their own choices – then…then he didn't need them.

Dropping back on his bed and stretching out, Luke put his hands behind his head and looked up at the ceiling, which loomed over him like a black storm. Outside a gentle rain had begun to fall and, because of the silence throughout the house, its pitter-patter against his window seemed louder and more insistent than it was, more like the impatient tapping of one's fingernails on the kitchen table. 'But apart from becoming a swan,' he asked himself, 'what would I like to be?' The question sounded strange as he rolled it around in his mind, because people don't normally turn into animals, and yet…and yet it was now a real and vital question to consider. He could follow the rest of the Cygnets and turn into a swan, and if he became dissatisfied with being such an animal, or if the Cygnets turned their backs on him for any reason, he could easily (or at least it seemed easy) turn back and live the rest of his days as a human. This would hardly be a bad thing, although it would be a wasted opportunity if being an animal, even for a few minutes, was really a great thing, was really as great as they all made it out to be. But forgetting the Cygnets for a few minutes, he continued, 'what kind of animal would I like to be if there was no reason why I couldn't choose to be anything I wanted?'

Trying to visualize a parade of possible choices, Luke suddenly remembered Butch, his golden retriever, whose collar was still in his top drawer. Butch was the greatest animal that had even lived – he would follow Luke when allowed out of the yard, and at night he would sleep next to Luke, against his legs, always ready to get up with Luke, always eager for Luke to walk him. Sometimes when Luke left the house to see the Cygnets, Butch would look through Luke's bedroom window to watch Luke disappear down the street or into the darkness. Luke jumped up and checked the window for marks made by the dog's nose, but it was either too dark to tell or else his mother had cleaned the window, and so he went back to bed, once again lying on his back and contemplating the choice he had to make. Golden retrievers are the greatest animals in the world, he told himself, and he couldn't help wondering if by becoming such a dog, he could bring back at least the spirit of Butch. Of course, he told himself, moments before he fell asleep, it could be a big mistake not to follow the other Cygnets.

The next day, none of the Cygnets were at school. Someone mentioned they were sick, and this seemed reasonable since they had spent so much time in the cool water and could easily have a cold or something. Chuckling to himself when he heard the news ('serves them right,' he added with a slight sneer), Luke put the matter out of his mind and promised himself that he would speak to them when they returned. They were out the next day, too, but even this wasn't a complete surprise since he knew that the flu and colds take at least a couple of days to subside. But when they were out the day after this and the day after that, Luke had become worried that their illnesses were more severe that he thought, and he regretted making the remark about serving them right. That evening, Luke decided to call them to find out their status and see what if anything he could do to help.

However, while he was becoming more and more concerned over their illnesses, he nevertheless harbored a slight suspicion that there was no sickness at all and that they had been spending their time at the lake…without him. Not only without him, but without having told him what they were doing or going to do. That was the most troubling thing of all, because they had never done such a thing – they always told one another where they were going and whether or not they would be in school, at the lake, or wherever. That's why they were the Cygnets – because they kept each other informed and because they all made sure that if one was at the lake, then the others would be there, too. 'No,' Luke told himself as he dialed Lu's number. 'No, thinking such thoughts is the same as being disloyal to everyone, and he was not disloyal. Like a dog, he was loyal to his best friends. But after he contacted the homes of Lu, Press, and Dana and was informed that they were either at this place or that (obviously, no one knew of their absence from school), Luke changed his mind, because it was clear that it was not he who had been disloyal, but them – none of them had bothered to contact him about their plans, an act which at that moment almost seemed as if they had severed their connections with him.

Despite all his doubts, it was hard for Luke to believe that things had come to this, and on Friday when Jimmy reminded him that he had lost his girlfriends, Luke lashed out at him uncharacteristically and had even pushed the boy to the ground. Luckily, Jimmy backed away, doing little else than calling him a sissy, and when Luke returned home that evening and went into his room, he fell face down on his bed and began to cry. He had lost his friends and had done something to another boy that he had never done before. Life at that point held little value for Luke, and there was certainly no reason for him to ever again visit the lake.

Chapter Eighteen - Luke was right

Luke was right. Each morning the girls left for school, and each afternoon they returned from school, their backpacks filled with books and homework, and not once during this time did they actually step foot on school property. No one, except the girls themselves, had any idea that they were not attending school and were, instead, spending their days at the lake, paddling this way and that, bobbing their heads up and down, and living their lives as pristine white swans. And they spent every second of this time with Iowa, who rarely reverted to human form and who now lived at the lake because, as they all knew, she didn't have a human home to go to.

Not once during this time did the girls regret missing school or feel guilty for the subterfuge they used to keep family, friends, and authorities from finding out how they spent their days. Perhaps it didn't matter if someone found out, because they could easily assume the shape of a swan and no one would be able to associate the animal with their human shape. In fact, at various times throughout the week, each of the girls considered leaving their human forms permanently and spending the rest of their days with Iowa, who was a wonderful friend and who now lived the most amazing life, a life that was inconceivable to them just a few days ago. Indeed, the girls were beginning to realize that nothing was more amazing, more compelling, than experiencing life through the senses – the sights, sounds, and smells – of a swan. True, the world through a swan's eyes wasn't quite as colorful, and the birds were incapable of moving with the speed and agility of human beings, but what they could do far exceeded human capabilities and made the Cygnets wonder why they would want to return to human form except perhaps to alleviate their parents' and siblings' concerns over their absence.

If swans couldn't perceive colors as well as humans, their ability to perceive shapes and movements more than made up for any minor chromatic deficiency. To a swan, for example, the lake's currents appeared as glistening, sinuous waves that gently rocked back and forth from one shore to the next, and when the currents were disturbed (the flutter of a fish's tail or the impact of a dry leaf on the water's surface), small pulsations were returned that indicated the direction and shape of the object causing the disturbance. Swans cannot perceive all the sounds that human ears can distinguish, but on the other hand they have the ability to isolate everything they can hear – removing or erasing the drone of car engines, the clatter of footsteps on the ground, and even the cacophony of human speech – so that they can hone in on specific noises, perceiving them clearly even if they were made in the midst of a raging storm. More amazing than any human capability is a swan's ability to identify objects, other swans, and even people by their smell. The size and shape of a swan somewhere miles away could easily be identified by its specific and pleasant smell, just as a single blade of green grass could be separated from all the other blades surrounding it by its own unique odor. Even the movements – yes, the movements -- of small minnows emitted an identifying smell in addition to their pulsations, preventing the girls from ever going hungry while on the lake. Dana was particularly impressed by the way she could hold her head under water (her tail high in the air) and, watching and smelling the undulations of small fish as they darted for safety, scoop them up before they could pass beyond her shadow. The fish tasted good, too, better than any meal her mother had ever cooked, which in itself was surprising because she loved her mother's cooking and hated anchovies.

From the very beginning of their adventure, Press, Lu, and Dana had established a routine that rarely varied. Each morning, they would arrive at the edge of the lake where Iowa would be waiting for them (she would be floating in the water about ten feet from shore), and then within seconds after changing into white swans they would plop, plop, plop into the water and, when it was deep enough, swish across the surface, their tails shaking, to meet Iowa. Without a word between them, they would paddle single file to the center of the lake and then splash and bounce into one another, sometimes intertwining their long necks or bouncing their heads up and down, after which they would resume the splashing and bouncing. Later in the morning, for variety's sake, they would circumnavigate the lake, after which they would gather in the center and, dipping their heads in and out of the water to splash their backs and the backs of their necks, sometimes increasing the spray by flapping their large wings. The sun was almost directly overhead by this time and, without a single, visible clue as to what they were going to do next, they would fall into a line and head toward the shore, where they would waddle out of the water, turn, and ease themselves down onto the wet earth, twisting their heads backwards to bury them into their wings. Beneath the warm, golden glow of the sun, they would sleep contentedly for an hour or two. Press was usually the first to wake -- she rarely slept long and was always looking for some way to exercise – and, after stretching and flapping her wings, she would waddle back into the water and, with a slight splash as she settled on the water's surface, inadvertently waking the others, who would sleepily follow suit. Eating, which accompanied most of their activities, was a relatively simple affair – you just stretched your head beneath the surface of the water, tilting your tail upward to obtain the maximum reach, and then gobbled minnows and whatever else came your way. It was all good and filling.

Now, while they were on the water, they always seemed to be engaged in something – a swim across the lake, a promenade around the perimeter of the lake, an occasional foray onto the shore to eat some grass – the Cygnets still made time to relax and float aimlessly near the center of the lake. The first time they did this, eyes closed, heads bent against their breasts, the sensation was slightly unnerving – they felt as if they were floating in air – but after a few times, the sensation became natural and they began to think and experience the world not as human beings but as swans, nearly forgetting that unlike Iowa, they had to revert to human form and go home in the late afternoon, as if nothing out of the ordinary had happened. Even when experiencing the near absence of conscious thought, they had a swan's sense of time (albeit one informed by human necessities), and never once failed to wake up on time and return home when expected. But what was truly unexpected (and a swan expects few things) was the mental shock that filled their heads when they donned their human forms. A swan's head is not buzzing with things remembered, problems to be solved, or distractions of every possible shape, sound, and motion. It is calm, unthinking, and free from almost everything except physical sensation or stimulation; the Cygnets were indeed amazed by their experiences as swans, but they could only feel this amazement in their human form – as a swan, it was simply life as a swan. It may have been that human shock that, when they looked back at their experiences in the water, led them to value their lives as swans as highly, if not more highly, than their lives as human beings.

One evening – it must have been Thursday or Friday – there was a general reluctance to change from swan to human and leave the special life behind, even though they could return any time they wanted. None of them were truly ready to sever most of their connections with humans like Iowa did, and yet it wouldn't have taken much for them to forgo being humans for a day or two, or more. Of all people, it was Dana who, after reverting to human form, asked the others (including Iowa, who didn't change back) if they might at least stay the night as a swan. "No one will miss us, and, really, do we care if they do?"

"What about our families?" Lu asked.

"What do you mean? This is our family, and there is no sense abandoning it every evening to go back to some place that doesn't make sense and is filled with such nastiness that sometimes I feel like doing away with myself."

"Come on," Press said and began walking back through the trees and along the path. "We all feel this way when we change back, but at least for now we have to return to our other families. The time will come soon enough when we can go about our business as we see fit."

"But Iowa did it," she pushed back. "Iowa did it, and she doesn't have the slightest regret."

"No, but then she doesn't have parents either, and if she were to attempt to go back, the Smiths would be all over her, and that would be the last we'd ever see of her."

"Maybe you're right," she sighed. "But I'm truly beginning to hate human life." No one responded, because they were all beginning to hate human life in one way or another.

No one thought about Luke. Normally, Luke would have been as much on their thoughts as any other member of the Cygnets, but for some reason the intellectual blankness of swan life eroded or smoothed out certain aspects of their memories and emotions even after they resumed human shapes. Unquestionably, they would have recognized Luke if he popped up, but the pull of existing in the moment, of setting aside one's past and future, unless it had to do with fear or hunger, was extraordinarily powerful and it induced a way of thinking that was difficult to shake. They loved Luke, they would have been thrilled to see him, but unless he suddenly appeared – especially in the shape of a swan -- he had no more relevance to them than the next day's homework.

Chapter Nineteen - Luke visited the lake once toward the end of the week

Luke had visited the lake once toward the end of the week, but not finding any obvious evidence of the presence of the Cygnets he quickly returned home. It was disconcerting, because he was certain they were there, somewhere, maybe in the shadows around the lake or in the woods, but since he refused to scour the area (he couldn't countenance the idea that they would hide from him), he quite reasonably assumed that the odds of overlooking them was quite good, even if they were no more than a few feet away. On Saturday, confident that they would be there and determined to find them even if he had to look into each shadow or under every bush, Luke went to the lake filled with the joy of having discovered something truly special that he was going share with the Cygnets and nobody else.

Throughout the short walk on the path, ducking his head now and then to avoid low-hanging branches and pausing briefly to empty a rock from his left shoe, Luke rehearsed in his mind what he would say to them and pictured how they would respond to what he had to say. A little melodramatic perhaps, he pictured Press, Dana, Lu, and Iowa standing in silence by the edge of the water while he explained his plans, after which each one of them following Iowa's lead (she would be standing slightly apart from the others, waiting for what she knew would come) would walk over to him and, individually, offer a heartfelt apology for having treated him so poorly. Naturally, he would forgive each one of them -- with a hard stare and then with a loving smile – and afterwards they would all resume their friendship (bad times now forgotten) as Cygnets. Luke was still somewhat anxious about how things would play out (what if they refused to assume human form?), although he was confident that if he was able to say and demonstrate what he needed to say and demonstrate, they would all come around in one way or other.

Luke began scanning the surface of the water the very second he reached the clearing (it was obvious they were not in the clearing or anywhere else immediately in sight). But because the morning's light was clear and exceptionally bright, he was able to see only small portions of the lake at a time and was forced to shield his eyes from the brilliant glare, which at times made the water seem like a mirror reflecting the sun's light. By holding his right hand over his eyes and peering intermittently through the cracks between his fingers, Luke was able to survey a fair amount of the lake without, however, viewing the lake as a whole.

Unfortunately, no matter how he positioned his fingers, no matter where he stood in the clearing, Luke was unable to locate anything that suggested the presence of swans or birds of any kind. But since he was positive they would be there (the Cygnets were always at the lake Saturday mornings), he continued to search the surface of the water over and over, from one side to the other and back again, each time trying to take in as much of the water's surface as he could with his increasingly sore, sun-spotted eyes. Realizing that he could adequately search only a fraction of the lake from the clearing, Luke walked half-way around the lake on the left – stomping through high grass and weeds, and meandering around thick, sloping trees some of whose branches reached down to touch their reflections reaching up to meet them – after which he retraced his steps and walked around the other half of the lake, avoiding the same kinds of obstacles – including large rocks and boulders that seemed to have been placed on the water's edge by a mad giant determined to prevent Luke from seeing the lake clearly from many angle – only to return to the clearing angry and disappointed because there were still no traces of the swans to be seen anywhere. "Where are they?" he asked himself and the open air again and again. In response, both he and the gentle breeze, which at times was indistinguishable from his own breathing, said just as frequently, "They have to be here. Where else could they be?"

Luke scoured the lake until his eyes ached and small spots danced across his vision, and then he walked through the grass and shrubs surrounding the clearing, kicking at clumps of grass big enough to hide a large bird before he tired and, demoralized, decided to give up. It had taken him nearly an hour (or so he judged) to arrive at the point at which he was ready to give up on them forever, or at least until tomorrow when he came back and resumed his search. Standing on the edge of the path, his back to the water, Luke was about to leave the park when he heard a horn-like sound emanating from the other side of the lake. Craning his head, turning toward the lake, and shading his eyes with his left hand, Luke listened intently for the sound while scanning the water's surface for something that could have made the sound. But as he strained every nerve to hear something – something other than waves tapping the shore or bugs chirping in the tall grass – there was nothing, no horn, no swans, just the stillness of the lake and the surrounding trees. Luke was about to write off the sound as an aberration of some sort – maybe it was a tree branch that had snapped -- when in the distance he caught sight of a white shape coming out of the shadows at the far side of the lake. It was a swan, and shortly after the appearance of this animal another followed in its wake, and then two more. One of the swans, the lead swan, turned and caught sight of Luke, who was quietly smiling at his discovery, and began swimming quickly toward him, the others following but at a slower, more leisurely pace.

Iowa continued to the shore while the others hung back some thirty feet or so from the shore, and stared expectantly at Luke and Iowa. Iowa walked up onto shore and then, in less than a few seconds, changed into her human shape. Once she stood up, she ran to Luke and hugged him tightly, something she never before attempted. Luke was taken aback, but luxuriated in the feeling that he was beginning to fear had been lost forever.

"I'm glad you came," Iowa said breathlessly, as if she had been exercising before Luke arrived.

"I came here a couple of days ago, too, but no one was here."

"That's surprising. We were here. Well, it doesn't matter. You're here now. Are you going to stay with us?" Luke didn't immediately grasp the meaning of her last sentence, in part because he noticed that the others were still keeping their distance.

"Why aren't they coming over, too?"

Iowa glanced over her shoulder at them and then back at Luke. "I don't know. They're swans, and swans can sometimes be hesitant. It's nothing."

"You didn't hesitate."

"I've been doing this for a lot longer than they have."

"But I thought we were all family, and there shouldn't be any hesitation among family, right?"

Iowa smiled and didn't try to answer Luke's question. "Yes, we are family, Luke."

This didn't satisfy him, and strange new feelings of resentment and anger against the others suddenly rose in his mind. He knew Iowa was telling the truth, but that still didn't change the fact that the others were staying away from him, that something was happening which made them hesitant – or simply uninterested – to associate with him. But what had he done? And why couldn't someone simply say what the problem was so that it could be resolved?

Iowa took Luke by the hands and looked into his eyes. "Do you want to change?" she asked, smiling at him.

He couldn't help smiling back at her. "Yes, I do, very much. In fact, I…but is it necessary to be a swan?"

"No, of course not. It never was. I told you that. Maybe it would make things easier, but you can be anything you want. So what do you want to be?"

"I don't want to be a swan, but if I don't become one I'm afraid the others will have nothing to do with me." Luke felt funny saying such things to Iowa, but he couldn't help it because of the emotions now roiling inside him – the fear of loss, the desire to hold on desperately, and, of course, his attraction to Iowa – which at the same time filled his eyes with tears.

"No, that's not the case. We'll love you no matter what you are. Naturally, we're hoping that you will become something like us, but whatever you choose is up to you, and we'll support it."

"Then why are they swimming away?"

It was true. While they were talking, the others had begun slowly swimming toward the center of the lake, and it appeared that it would take something extraordinary to bring them back.

Iowa glanced at them without releasing Luke's hands. "I don't know. They'll be back as soon as you change. Trust me. Now, what it is going to be, mister? Swan or goose or what?"

"Look, if I change into something, can I ever change back? I mean, can I change my mind and be something else?"

"No, I'm afraid not. Once you've chosen, you can make no other choice, other than to go back to being human. What is it? You don't have to be a swan."

Luke hesitated, and then pulled away from Iowa and turned his back to her. "Are you sure?"

"Yes. My mother was very explicit, and I tried once and it didn't work. In fact, it made me very ill, and so I wouldn't try it once you've changed. It could...well, just don't do it."

Luke turned back to Iowa, and there was a scared look in his eyes. "I've already changed. Your instructions were perfect."

"Wonderful. Are you ready to go into the water?"

"I changed a few days ago. Look, no one was around, and no one was talking to me, just like now." He motioned in their direction. A strange, troubled look came over Iowa's face.

"So what are you?"

"I think I made a mistake. I should have become a swan or a duck or something like that, but, I don't know, no one would talk to me, and when they did, it was all about how great it was to be a swan. Maybe I was a little angry at being left out, maybe a little lonely being without my friends, and so...well, I changed into a golden retriever. You know how much I like those dogs."

Iowa was serious for a moment and then laughed. Luke stepped back. "I'm not laughing at you. I'm only laughing because it's okay. It's not a big deal. You can be anything you want, and we will still love you."

"They won't. They're already hiding from me, as if they suspect something."

"Nothing of the kind. Now, show me what you've become." She stepped back and, spreading her feet and crossing her arms, waited for Luke to change. He didn't disappoint her, for within thirty seconds, he became a large, boisterous golden retriever, bouncing up and down and either licking Iowa's hands or trying to jump up on her.

Iowa couldn't help laughing and even petted him and told him to sit when he became a little too rambunctious. Iowa had never owned a dog, and the prospect of having one so close momentarily filled her with the desire to play with it. Picking up a stick, she threw it toward the trees. Luke, after following its trajectory, sprang toward it and galloped back with it, laying it at her feet. Once again, she threw the stick, this time as far as she could, and before it hit the ground Luke was charging after it, a few seconds later dropping it at her feet. This went on three or four more times, each time Luke barked with enthusiasm, until Iowa realized that the game had to stop for a few minutes at least so she could get the others to come over and greet Luke. When Luke came back the final time, panting and barking for more, Iowa reached down and patted him on the head and side and told him over and over that he was a good boy. Luke, however, had trouble settling down and kept jumping on Iowa or else wanting to charge back into the trees to retrieve another stick. Somehow, though, she managed to calm him a little, while he sat in front of her, his eyes fixed on hers and his tail moving back and forth in the dirt and creating a fan-like pattern on the ground; and when she was certain that he was paying attention to her words, she explained to him that the others needed to see him and get used to his new appearance. At the same time, she was beginning to have misgivings, because she didn't know how they would be able to interact with one another, since dogs and birds have little in common.

"Now, settle down, Lukie, settle down," she said, trying earnestly to hold Luke steady by pressing down on his head with her right hand. She glanced over her right shoulder and, pointing with her left hand, said, "Look at Press, Lu, and Dana, Lukie, do you see them?" Iowa had instinctively begun calling Luke by this term of endearment, perhaps hoping that this would be enough to change his behavior so as to bridge the gap between what he had become and what they were. She told herself that there was no reason they shouldn't all get along, since they had loved one another for years and would love one another for years more. Iowa hoped half praying that no one would let their outward form dictate their feelings. 'We love each other and that will never change,' she assured herself.

Chapter Twenty - Luke stood up

Luke stood up and, still wagging his tail, craned his neck around her legs to get a clear look at the others. For whatever reason, they suddenly turned their backs and began swimming away, a clear sign that they had severed their relationship with him. In an instant, Luke bounded away from Iowa and charged out to the lake, splashing into the water and dashing maybe ten feet from the shore. Refusing to stand still despite Iowa's admonitions, he jumped up and down creating white, foamy waves in the water surrounding him, and barked loudly and vigorously to signal his presence and his desire to play with them. The swans, however, continued to swim away, which only increased Luke's frenzy and their fear of what he would do if they came near. They were all animals, of course, and at that moment none of them could bridge the gap between their current shapes and former selves.

"Luke, quiet, quiet!" Iowa shouted at Luke, which didn't have any effect other than to increase the urgency of his bouncing, splashing, and barking.

"Press, Lu, it's all right, come over. Dana, please come over and talk to Luke. Guys, don't leave," she cried. "Change back." Iowa thought that she could straighten things out, if only Luke would calm down and the others would return both to the shore and their human selves. It might even be fun to play with Luke for a while before he returned to his human form. But before she had a chance to calm everyone and get the situation under control, Luke bolted and raced around the lake to where the swans were swimming. They noticed his charging presence just as he reached their side, maybe fifty feet from the shore, and in a fright they turned and began swimming toward the center of the lake. Luke, fearing that they were going to evade him by going to the other shore, charged furiously back, his sides breathing heavily, foam frothing in his mouth, barking frantically. Perhaps it was anger over their clear rejection of him, as well as his innate tendencies as a dog to chase and bark, but whatever it was Luke was now completely out of control and nothing that Iowa screamed could slow him down.

The others had just about reached the shore when Luke arrived, but this time when they turned to swim away from him, he dove into the water and began swimming toward them.

"Luke," Iowa screamed frantically, "Stop, stop. Press, change for God's sake!"

Luke was about ten feet from the frightened swans, when he suddenly turned around and slowly swam back to shore. Swimming and running and his nonstop barking had exhausted him, and the moment he was within reach of them, he felt as though he was going to collapse and drown. When he reached shore, he walked out the water and collapsed on his side, his tongue hanging out and sides moving heavily up and down.

Iowa ran over to where Luke was lying on the ground. At about the same time she reached Luke and kneeled down next to him to see if he was all right, Press had reappeared in human form. The others remained as they were. Press, however, didn't get any closer to the shore, and from her position in the lake (the water was up to her chest) – which was close enough to communicate effectively with Iowa and Luke on shore -- she began screaming at Luke and accusing him of all kinds of things.

"What's the matter with you?" she screamed several times. "Are you trying to kill us? You're insane. You're disgusting. I can't believe that you have such vile manners. You're not a dog; you're a rat. You're a snake. Why don't you leave us alone? Isn't it clear that we don't want you here with us? Didn't you get the clue? What do we have to say to make you leave us alone?"

Luke was still on the ground while Press was saying all this, and Iowa was attending to him, petting him, saying soothing things, trying to make him comfortable because she thought he had somehow hurt himself. She didn't approve of his behavior, but at the same time she recognized that his behavior was normal for a dog, and she didn't believe that he really wanted to hurt anyone even accidentally. Iowa was shocked, however, when she heard what Press was screaming, because it was uncalled-for and absolutely not the way one treats family or even friends. While she felt that Press's reaction was the result of animal instincts that had not yet worn off when she changed back to her human form, she was nevertheless disturbed by the ugliness of Press's face as she screamed at Luke and disgusted by the degree of her anger – it was simply inexcusable regardless of the circumstances that gave rise to it. Turning her shoulders to face Press directly (she was going to tell Press to shut up and demand that she apologize to Luke for maligning him unjustly), Iowa suddenly felt Luke's fur slipping from her fingers and in an instant he was free and on his feet. Luke dashed away from the clearing and into the woods without looking back.

"What is the matter with you?" Iowa shouted to Press. "He wasn't going to hurt anyone. He was feeling for the first time what it was like to be a dog…"

"Maybe you didn't see him well enough. If you hadn't been here, he would have continued after us. Why did he choose to be a mad dog, anyway? Wasn't there something else he could have chosen? If he had the least feeling for us, he could have changed into a swan or something compatible, not this…this monster. He just showed us that he doesn't care for us, and we don't need him, either. We never did."

Without waiting for Iowa to respond – and Iowa was too shocked by what had happened and Press's ugly words to respond immediately – Press reverted to a swan and swam out to the others, who were visibly shaken by what had happened.

Iowa watched them swim together toward one of the outer sections of the lake. She couldn't explain things now, assuming that they would even believe her, certainly not while they were swans, and it was with some grave misgivings that she, too, turned into a swan and swam out to the others. If nothing else, she told herself, she could at least calm the others down, especially Lu, who seemed unusually shaken by the events.

Chapter Twenty-One - Except for Iowa, everyone as expected was at school

Except for Iowa, everyone as expected was at school Monday, and apart from the fact that Luke was no longer welcome among the Cygnets, everything appeared normal. Luke's friendly troublemaker, Jimmy, the boy who had taunted him about his girlfriends, noticed the change and became more friendly to Luke and, over the course of three days, was able to insinuate himself into Luke's company during lunch and other free times. He didn't mention the girls, who either ignored Luke or, whenever they noticed his presence, would feign indifference or simply scowl.

On Thursday, just as Jimmy got up from the lunch table that he had shared with Luke and some of the other boys (who had left earlier) and returned to class, Ms. Royce sat down and looked at Luke. Luke was not in Ms. Royce's class this quarter, but he had been last quarter and so he knew her fairly well.

"I see you're not eating lunch with your friends these days," she began without any preliminaries. Her face looked pleasant – he noticed the freckles across the bridge of her nose – and yet he couldn't help feeling that there was something serious behind her question. This was especially so when he noticed her small, slender fingers, all of which she interlaced and rested on the table in front of her.

"What? I had lunch with Jimmy and some of the other boys."

"You know what I mean. What's the problem?"

"Nothing. We had…well, I sometimes have lunch with other people. Besides, I am tired of having lunch with them, and I need a change, that's all." Luke felt nervous speaking to Ms. Royce, and his discomfort was compounded by his lying, which he feared she could detect.

"Very interesting. You've been close to Lu, Press, and Dana for how many years, and suddenly you're all acting like strangers? Doesn't make sense, does it?"

"I don't know what you mean," he replied avoiding her eyes but noticing the slight tremor in her right index finger.

"That's all right, no crime committed. But if you're having problems, you can always come to me. I've known all you kids for years, and even if I can only provide limited help, it's always good to get things off your chest. Do you understand what I'm saying?"

Luke nodded, and when she started to go, he felt like he had just weathered a great storm. Unfortunately, his relief was short lived, for just as she was getting up, she hesitated and sat back down. "May I ask you one more question? Have you seen Iowa lately?"

Luke could feel his body jerk at that question, but he refused to tell her the truth because he still felt loyalty to his friend, even though she spent all her time with the others and never once invited him to the lake. Not that it really mattered, or so he told himself. "No, I haven't. Did she come back? I thought she was living with the Smiths."

"No, she never went to the Smiths and, as far as I know, she never left town."

"Really, where is she staying?"

"I thought you might know." Ms. Royce had a way of asking questions that implied that she knew far more than she was letting on. He couldn't be certain, in this instance, whether she really knew something or was simply fishing for information. In any event, he wasn't going to tell her and get Iowa into trouble.

"No. I wish I did. She's a good friend."

"Not like the other girls, right?"

"No, it's not like that. I think I am late. May I leave to go to class?"

"Sure. I'm sure you knew the Smiths left some time ago. Between you and me, I think she's still here. And you know what else, there's something different about her, something that's helping her hide from everyone except, I suppose, a handful of friends." She looked intently at Luke, and he couldn't help observing how dark her eyes were and how cold her expression had become. Normally, she always had an open, welcome facial expression, but she suddenly looked different, and he didn't like how different she had become. Even her hands, which again were on the table, were different – they looked like fists.

"I...I don't know what you mean. How would she be different?"

"I don't know, but I saw it in her eyes. I can see a lot of things in people's eyes, even yours." Involuntarily, Luke turned away from Ms. Royce's intense gaze. "Do you want to know something else? The last time I looked at her, she reminded me of an animal. There was something in her that wasn't quite human, that was cold and fierce...like...have you ever looked into an animal's eyes? If you really look into them, not at the movement of the skin around the eyes or even the color of the irises, but into the pupils, you'll see how cold and lifeless they are. Even a dog's eyes are cold, as if all the feeling that we attribute to them is really only a reflection of our own desires. It's like looking into a mirror and only seeing what we want to see. Did you know I used to have a dog? He was always happy to see me, but one day I really looked at him and I could see that he wasn't really much of a friend at all. Something wasn't right. I don't know where I'm going with this. But you need to tell Iowa, if you ever see her again, that changing back and forth can produce permanent alterations that she can't control. I would tell your friends, but I'm afraid that they wouldn't understand, not when life's so much fun. Do you understand me?"

Luke didn't say anything, while Ms. Royce got up and walked back to the classrooms. He watched her slim shape as it disappeared around the corner, and he couldn't help feeling that there was something strange about her, something maybe unearthly. He couldn't explain it, not even in words that he could understand, and yet it was there, amorphous and indescribable, and at the same time disturbing, as if there were some kind of trouble inherent both in her presence and her words. Indeed, her words troubled him, because she seemed to imply that she knew everything – what happened to the Cygnets, how they changed, and maybe even how he changed – everything, that is, except Iowa's whereabouts. It was funny that she knew everything and yet didn't seem to have a clue where Iowa was hiding, or at least spending her days. Maybe she knew but was holding back to get him to confess.

But why would she want him to confess, and what would she want him to confess to? Barking too much and chasing the swans? That was nuisance behavior, as his father would have said, but certainly nothing that required a confession. It didn't make sense, and the more Luke puzzled over what she had said, the more uncomfortable he became until he started to worry that someone – probably Iowa herself – had done something that was truly bad and that could get everyone in trouble. Grabbing his head and forcing his fingers through his short hair, Luke debated with himself as to whether he should go to Iowa and tell her about the conversation with Ms. Royce (and, if he went, he could be leading anyone who was following him right to where Iowa could be found), or simply keep quiet and assume that his concerns were imaginary, the result of an emotional state brought about by having been separated from his best friends, his family, as Iowa reaffirmed. On the other hand,

Luke did want to see Iowa again – he wanted to apologize to her and explain what had just happened – and maybe, he reasoned, it might be worth the risk, especially if he took extra precautions to make sure that no one was following him. Of course, he was likely to encounter the other Cygnets, who would now do their best to keep Iowa away from him, and yet he suddenly felt confident that he could find a way around them, even if he didn't have the slightest idea at the moment how to accomplish that feat. Well, he wouldn't attempt to see her unless he was certain that it was completely safe to do so.

Luke didn't visit the lake that weekend. On Saturday, he accepted an invitation to spend the day at Jimmy's house. When he arrived, he recognized a half dozen other boys from school, and for the rest of the afternoon he enjoyed himself as he hadn't in months, maybe even longer than that. Naturally, it was a different kind of fun than he had experienced with the Cygnets – it was louder (most of the boys liked yelling) and more aggressive (shoving and wrestling were acceptable), and it was clear that he didn't have to worry whether he offended someone or did something that would cause some tears – and he began to think that he was as happy, if not more so, with Jimmy and the boys that with the Cygnets, even Iowa. The boys spent the afternoon playing war games, hiding and pretending to shoot one another, after which they told crude jokes. Luke had had such fun that he invited Jimmy and the boys to his house the next day, and they continued many of the games they had begun at Jimmy's.

Toward the end of the week, Jimmy and Luke became fast friends, and a circle of boys began gathering around them so that by Friday, Luke had enough friends and lunch companions, which more than made up for his expulsion from the Cygnets. Still, he hadn't forgotten his conversation with Ms. Royce, and every time he saw her, every time he thought about Iowa, he couldn't help wondering if he were remiss for not saying something to Iowa. It would have been convenient to convey what had happened to Press and the others, but he was positive that they wouldn't listen to him and, even if they did hear what he had to say, they probably wouldn't have said anything to Iowa because...because they were just like that, mean spirited and not interested in disturbing their special lives by mentioning him. 'What should I do?' Luke asked himself several times, each time alone, in his room, and looking outside into the dark, faceless night.

Chapter Twenty-Two - One night, three weeks after speaking to Ms. Royce

One night, three weeks after speaking to Ms. Royce, who eyed him intently every time she passed him in the hallway, Luke decided to sneak out of the house, go to the lake, and tell Iowa. It was doubtful that Press and the others would be there, and so it would be easy to speak to her alone and see her again. And he wanted to see her again. He was hopeful that she could forgive his actions as a dog and that they could now develop a good friendship of some kind. But what he truly didn't understand was that Ms. Royce's warning applied to him, too, although he was much safer than the others because he had changed only a few times and never remained in animal form for more than a few hours at a time, if that.

Luke listened intently for signs that his parents had gone to bed and were sleeping. Since their bedroom was next to his, Luke could always tell when his parents were in their room and whether or not they were sleeping. The clearest sign that they were asleep was his father's snoring, which sounded like a rasp being pulled across a piece of resistant wood (and sometimes the resistance was such that the rasp would explode, only to re-form seconds later and continue its futile effort), and Luke knew that by that time his mother had been quietly sleeping for some time prior. His mother was rarely up or awake after his father. It was nearly midnight when he recognized the rasp, the explosion, and the flutter (an inconsistent yet telltale sign of his father's slumber), and for good measure the occasional rattle of the headboard on his parents' bed, which cried out every time his father, a very large man, shifted his weight and position to free up his nasal cavities for more rasping.

Getting quietly out of bed, Luke tiptoed to the window and hesitated, looking outside as if he had expected his father or mother to show up suddenly and spoil his plans. While Luke knew it was unlikely that his parents would wake up before morning, his subterfuge (he was not, for the most part, a disobedient boy) set him on edge and made him especially cautious. Since Luke's room was on the main floor of the house (there was only a small guest room on the second floor), sneaking out through his window was quite simple, literally only a matter of sticking his toe out of the open window, stretching it and the rest of his leg over the bottom of the frame, and stretching until he could feel the soft grass outside. If he fell, if he slipped and toppled head first out of the window, it was unlikely that he would incur anything more significant than a slight bruise because the ground was so close. In fact, he had crawled out the window many times before, although rarely at night and almost never in defiance of his parents' rules that required him to stay inside at night, unless otherwise permitted. Nevertheless, once he opened the window (which, because it was unexpectedly stuck, burst open with a crash, forcing him to stand motionless for several minutes to be sure that no one heard the noise) and stretched his left leg outside and over the ground, the distance from the window to the ground unexpectedly seemed much farther than he had remembered it (from last week), and as he stretched, reaching out and down more than seemed reasonable, the whole house seemed to wake up and called attention to his crime -- the window creaked, the floor on which he was standing groaned, and, if that weren't enough, a cool wind picked up outside and blew some of the tree limbs against the house, making a loud knocking that should have awoken anyone in the neighborhood. Luke hesitated and began to reconsider his plan, wondering if he should postpone it for another, less complicated evening, or abandon it altogether. His apprehensions eased somewhat when, despite the unearthly racket going on around him, the familiar rasp started up, the headboard rattled, and there was a flutter. Taking a deep, confident breath, he stretched his foot to its limit and found soft ground, and a second later he was outside standing on the grass, breathing in the cool, moist air.

Once free from the house, Luke became apprehensive again, fearing that his father had heard his escape or that his mother had not been sleeping at all and had been listening to his efforts to sneak out the window, and any second one or both of them would walk out of the shadows engulfing his house and the neighborhood and force him back into his room, where he would have the night to wonder what sort of punishment awaited him. Luke hesitated, listening through the breeze for signs that someone might be awake and straining his eyes to see in the shadows that filled the trees and surrounded the house evidence that someone was right that very moment walking toward him. Seconds later, Luke was on his way, walking quietly down the sidewalk that led to the park and, once over the small barrier at the end of the walk, jogging down the path and heading toward the lake. Although the moon was bright and bathed the top of the forest in a bright, silvery light, the path beneath the trees was still dark, making it difficult at times for him to follow without stumbling over a dead branch or stepping abruptly into a leaf-covered rock or hole.

If sneaking out of the house had been exciting, the prospect of seeing Iowa was even more thrilling, especially because he had something important to tell her that, if he understood Ms. Royce correctly, could have serious consequences. Unfortunately, he didn't know what those consequences were – maybe Iowa would know – and he wasn't confident that he could convey the underlying meaning of Ms. Royce's words adequately, since she didn't exactly spell out her meaning. Still, Luke was hopeful that Iowa would listen to him, even if he was unable to answer all her questions (she was certain to have lots of questions), but he could easily imagine her objections. 'So, she asked about me. If she knew where I was, she didn't need to ask. Besides, I know the consequences – the Smiths – and there's no way I'm going to live with them or move out of this area. And I don't have to.' And, ultimately, she would be right, unless Ms. Royce had the power to change into something else and therefore knew something that neither he nor Iowa knew or could understand. But that didn't exactly make sense. If Ms. Royce was able to be an animal, then she could have said something more directly (if being an animal indeed made a difference) instead of talking around the subject like a fake fortune teller. There was something else, however, something potentially more important than anything Ms. Royce had to say or do. Luke was apprehensive when he thought about it, and he wasn't at all certain that Iowa would listen to him after he gave her that piece of news.

Luke stopped and stood quietly, listening for something in the sounds of the leaves as they rattled in the trees or for something else whose presence would silence the peepers and crickets. Although it was difficult to see through the dark shadows surrounding the trees, his hearing seemed especially acute and more than made up for the temporary deficit of his eyesight. Turning his head this way and that, holding his breath so that the sounds of his body would not conflict with the sounds of the night, Luke turned his ears in every direction and mentally examined every sound that might be out of the ordinary before tentatively concluding, several minutes later, that he was mistaken about the sounds and that he was in fact alone in the dark night. Still, something inside him wasn't willing to rest on this evidence and whispered in his ear that he was not alone and that he was being followed, whether he could hear it or not. This voice was persuasive enough that every few feet or so, he would stop and listen to the forest before starting again. Sometimes he could hear faint noises that resembled echoes made as his shoes slapped the hard dirt, which was perhaps not surprising at this time of night, and yet something was not quite right about these echoes because they didn't uniformly follow the movements of his feet. Every time he stopped, though, the echoes stopped, too, and so after a while he chalked it off to his increasing nervousness and to the sound of his heart beating. Besides, who would be following him, and what purpose would they have, since he had given no one advance warning of his intentions?

As soon as Luke arrived at the clearing next to the lake, he looked up and down the shore, half of which looked almost like it did in the daylight, and then across the surface of the lake. The moon cast its silvery glow across the center of the lake to where he stood on the shore, and he could clearly see the calm ripples of the water as a slight breeze forced the water toward the shore. One the other side, however, where large trees curved and hung over the water, the lake was engulfed in a deep, impenetrable gloom, for only the tops of the trees were clearly outlined by the light. Everything except for the small waves and the slight noise they made as they washed up on shore was still and quiet, and the noises that had accompanied him to the lake were now thankfully gone. Luke didn't see anything. He squinted his eyes, he looked carefully at anything that didn't appear to be made of leaves and twigs, and he listened for telltale signs of life, bird life, which would indicate that Iowa was somewhere nearby. He even walked part of the way around the lake and then back, hoping to see Iowa somewhere, anywhere. But there was nothing.

He had been at the lake's edge for perhaps ten minutes when he called out her name in a loud whisper. He didn't know why he needed to whisper, since it was clear that no one was around, and yet he couldn't bring himself to call out her name and disturb the night. He did this several times, turning his head in every direction, but there was no response, save for a couple of disturbed starlings or whatever they were that flew out of the trees.

After a while with no response and no sighting of Iowa, Luke resigned himself to the reality that Iowa was not here and that he would probably never see her again. The thought filled him with an inexpressible sadness that made him want to try again and again to locate her on the lake or in the woods surrounding the lake. He wasn't ready to let her go, and yet no matter what he did, he couldn't locate her – she was gone. With his heart heavy, he noticed a flat rock on the shore and, picking it up and holding onto its edge, he sailed it across the lake where it bounced on the water's silvery surface ten times before sinking. There is something positive about personal challenges – such as skipping a rock across the surface of a lake – that can buoy one's spirits (or at least occupy one's thoughts) during stressful times like this one. Luke realized that there was no reason to stay at the lake, especially at this time of night, but before he could return home he had to see if he could bounce another rock off the lake's surface eleven times. After succeeding with that, he challenged himself to achieve twelve times, and then thirteen times. Luke had sailed perhaps twenty rocks when he finally stood up to leave. Taking one last look at the lake – and, for some reason, he thought that he might never again visit it – he noticed something strange in the distance, near where the trees were the thickest and darkest.

Initially, he wasn't entirely certain that he could see anything, because the shape was faint and often disappeared into the darkness or was replaced by other undulating shapes that after a few seconds were clearly the effects of the shifting light, the soft breeze, and his desire to see something. But as he continued straining his eyes, he notice a vague, ghost-like cloud floating just above the surface of the water that seemed to be separating itself from the darkness surrounding it, and as he observed it, trying his best to make out its shape, he soon became aware that it was becoming clearer, more distinct, and, moreover, was moving toward him. Within seconds, the cloud had resolved into a swan -- it was still somewhat indistinct, but there was no mistaking its ghostly white shape for anything other than a swan – and the clearer it became, the more convinced he was that it was Iowa, since there were no other swans or clouds on the lake and this one was swimming toward him. The closer she got to him, the clearer she became until she was maybe thirty feet from him and, by that time, he didn't have the slightest doubt that it was the very person or animal he sought. Luke was not surprised that she didn't change into human form, because she still had some of the lake to negotiate before reaching the shore. He smiled and waved to her, and something suggested (the way she looked at him, moving her head up and down with the movements of her paddling) that she was acknowledging him and was looking forward to seeing him as much as he was looking forward to seeing her.

Chapter Twenty-Three - Luke began to feel uneasy

Luke, however, began to feel uneasy as Iowa approached. He told himself that he didn't have any reason feel this way, since he had taken every precaution to ensure that he wasn't followed (which was little more than coming to the lake at night), and yet he couldn't shake the feeling that Iowa was in danger and that he alone could save her. Unfortunately, because his normally vivid imagination was particularly dull at that moment, he couldn't come up with a single reason to justify his uneasiness and hence couldn't take steps to protect Iowa if indeed she was in danger. Turning briefly away, Luke scanned the surface of the lake surrounding Iowa, who was now bathed in the silvery light from the moon, and then turned toward the trees at the far side of the lake. Nothing seemed unusual or a potential source of danger -- there was the lake, the clearing on this side of the lake, the trees at the far side of the lake, and the tall, dark grasses that seemed to float in the air on either side of the lake – but as he glanced at Iowa, who was inching closer and closer to the shore, and once more at the dark grasses, Luke sensed that the problem was here, only a short distance away.

"They're fireflies," he told himself , as he caught sight of the pinpricks of yellowish light emanating from the grass, and then changed his mind because they didn't act like fireflies. Fireflies move up and down, and their fires rage brilliantly for a few seconds before fading into oblivion. Luke could still remember promising himself when he was much younger that one day he would fly over the lake in a rocket ship and, looking through the ship's small, circular porthole, count all the brilliant little bugs, which would look like tiny stars in a black sky, rising and dying near the lake. But these bugs didn't move at all, or barely at all, and they certainly didn't fade away after a few precious moments. They were stationary, hovering over the tops of the grasses in pairs, as if one couldn't exist without the other, and their light was more like dying embers whose glow fluctuated only when you changed your position. Luke kept his eyes on both Iowa and the strange lights, and when she was only a few feet from the shore, all but two of the lights abruptly disappeared. The two that remained, however, somehow turned into a pair of large, gleaming eyes and within seconds a large animal bounded from the grasses about twenty feet away and charged toward Iowa.

Luke didn't have time to react when the animal galloped past him and, leaping into the water, splashed over to Iowa and grabbed the swan by the wing. The swan hadn't had time to react either and, by the time the animal reached her and grabbed her wing, it was too late. The animal pulled the helpless swan to the shore.

The animal, which proved to be a large dog, continued to pull the now-struggling swan away from the water into the woods.

Luke, having recovered from the shock of seeing the animal come out of nowhere, ran after it, wildly screaming Iowa's name as he ran. Luckily, Luke's screaming and his mad rush toward the dog clearly startled the animal, and it released the swan and jumped back several feet. Eyeing its prey, the dog nevertheless kept its distance while Luke ran to the swan and tried to help it struggle back to its feet. By the time the swan was finally on its feet again, Luke was surrounded by Lu, Dana, and Iowa, each one in human form.

Luke was dumbfounded and glanced at each of them, trying to understand what they were doing here in human form and what they were telling him, and each of them seemed to be hollering something at him. He turned to the swan he thought was Iowa, but when he looked down at her, it was Press, who had also returned to her human shape. Her arm was bloodied but it didn't look seriously hurt, even though she was holding it tightly and wincing in pain. Luke took a step back and, as he stared at them, observing their faces twist and turn as their jaws bounced up and down furiously, he couldn't help wondering if he was dreaming, particularly because everything within his sight – the Cygnets, including the injured Press, the lake, the clearing, the surrounding grassy fields, the night sky, and the dog – was completely silent, surrounded as he was by a heavy, muffled nothingness that vibrated softly inside him. 'Maybe,' he was able to think while the strange pantomimes were being acted out in front of him, 'maybe I never left my room, and I will wake up in the morning and all this will be gone.' But just as he was about ready to pretend that it was all a bad dream, the muffled silence surrounding him suddenly dissolved and he could hear all their voices distinctly, which were now inexplicably holding him responsible for what had happened.

"What's the matter with you," Lu and Dana were screaming at him, and both pushed him out of the way to reach down and attend to Press.

"I thought it was Iowa…," he began to mutter incoherently.

"So that's why you tried to kill her?" someone else screamed at him.

"No, no, that's not it. I only came here to warn Iowa of something…"

"This is your idea of warning her? What, were you warning her to come to the shore to be eaten? My God, you're a monster." It was Lu who was loudest, and he couldn't believe the strange and erroneous things she and the others were saying.

"No, no, I didn't want to hurt anyone." He looked around and noticed Iowa standing in the distance out of the light. "I only came to help…," he tried to tell her, but he was interrupted by Press, who in a low hissing voice blamed him for bringing all the trouble with him.

"No, no," he retorted, turning to her. "You've got it all wrong…"

"If she's got it all wrong," Dana said, stepping over to Luke, "then why was Press practically killed?"

"How could you do such a thing?"

"I didn't touch her. I tried to save her from the dog," he gasped and pointed to where the dog had been standing. The dog, however, was gone, and in its place was Jimmy, visibly shocked at what he had done. "Why?" Luke gasped, staring at Jimmy. Jimmy, however, was too shaken to do anything except stand, his arms at his sides, and look blankly at everyone.

"Yes, you are right, Jimmy attacked Press," Iowa said calmly as she came out of the shadows. "But Jimmy was a dog, and there was no one else who could have taught him what I taught you. Why did you tell him?"

"What?" Luke couldn't believe his ears. Iowa, the one person sensible enough to understand what had happened, was now holding him responsible for Press's injuries, and he was the one person who had tried to save her. In fact, if it hadn't been for him, Jimmy might still be holding Press, and yet Iowa wanted to know why he told Jimmy as if that was the root cause of all these – their – problems. "I...I...," Luke stammered momentarily, conscious that everyone was looking at him, their faces filled with the contempt they felt for him. "I...yes, I showed him how to do it, and it was his choice to become a dog. But I didn't tell him to hurt anyone. Why would I do that? And why are you and everyone else blaming me for that? And the only reason I told him anything was because everyone was turning against me. You were all telling me that I couldn't be a Cygnet anymore, even if I did become... Look, Jimmy accepted me. He didn't care if..." Luke looked at Iowa, Jimmy, and then the girls. "I only wanted things to be the same. I didn't want anyone to get hurt. I…I…" Everyone, except Jimmy, was watching him, expecting him to say something else, expecting him to take the blame and leave. He turned to Jimmy. "Why?" he screamed. "Why?"

Luke's words pulled Jimmy out of his stupor. Standing, surrounded by the Cygnets, each one of them looking at him, their faces twisted in anger, Jimmy stepped away from them and, turning, fled into the woods and out of the park, without reverting to animal form.

"I'm sorry," Luke said, looking first at Iowa and then at the other Cygnets. The fact that Jimmy had fled seemed, in Luke's eyes, to have taken some of the responsibility off his shoulders, and so he tried to say something that would at least quell their anger. "I came here because Ms. Royce said something dangerous could happen…" He didn't finish, because everyone was now crowded around Press, who was holding her right arm and loudly moaning that it hurt.

Luke, now standing by himself, watching everyone fuss over Press, couldn't believe that everything he tried to do to protect Iowa – which no doubt would have protected the other Cygnets as well – had come to nothing, and instead of being welcomed back to the Cygnets, he was obviously being expelled from the group. Maybe someday Iowa would understand; maybe she would forgive him and tell the others that he only meant to help – that his actions, which were harmless, were in large measure a response to their own cruelties, which were intended to keep him out of their clique.

Maybe…but at that moment none of them, not even Iowa, were in the least bit interested in the truth or in anything he had to say about Ms. Royce, which he alone knew was important.

While Iowa was helping Press, soothing her injuries (which appeared to be little more than a few small scratches and welts and one shallow puncture) and calming her down (her moaning seemed disproportionate to her injuries and quite possibly designed to concentrate everyone's attention on her), she mulled over what she was going to say to Luke. Unlike the others, she knew that he wasn't responsible for what had happened to Press, and she felt bad that she hadn't said enough to make this clear or hadn't done enough to temper their anger toward Luke. Luke would never have done anything intentionally to hurt them or anyone else. Nevertheless, even though he wasn't directly responsible, he was at least indirectly responsible, for he had told somebody about changing and she had made it very clear that no one outside of the Cygnets was to know. "I told everyone not to say a word," she mumbled to herself, while the others continued fussing over Press and, at the same time, discussing what had happened and what could happen if Jimmy (or Luke, although they didn't mention his name) came back.

"If he hadn't opened his mouth," one of them said, as if Luke had fled with Jimmy, "none of this would have happened. No one would have been angry with him."

Iowa frowned without saying anything. It didn't immediately occur to her that Luke was listening to all the nonsense surrounding Press, especially because he had been standing a few feet away and all the noise should have sounded like an incomprehensible babble of geese, or swans. She intended to speak to him in a few minutes, making him understand the problems that could arise if Jimmy were to change again and, what would be worse, if he were to tell anyone else how to change. She didn't want to think about that, since she knew that there was very little she or anyone else could do now to change things. But just as she stepped back from Press, having had enough of her complaints and her bellyaching about being forced to postpose her participation in this or that sport, Iowa suddenly recalled something that Luke had said about Ms. Royce. Normally, Iowa wouldn't have cared what some teacher said, but for some reason the fact that it was Ms. Royce and not just any teacher troubled her, and she immediately turned around to demand more details from Luke. Luke was gone.

Chapter Twenty-Four - There was no school the next day

There was no school the next day, and the day after that was a holiday. Normally, Luke would have been eager to spend both days at the lake, but after everything that had happened there, not to mention the fact that he was no longer welcome among the Cygnets, the lake was practically the last place in the world that he wanted to visit. 'Really, what's the point of visiting the lake now?' he asked himself, as he was preparing to leave his house. 'They'll all be there, and when they see me, they'll turn their backs to me and do whatever they can to show their hatred for me.' But instead of staying at home and bemoaning his situation, he decided that the best thing for him to do was to go outside, clear his mind, and visit some friends, people who forgive and don't judge. Luke, as he closed the front door behind him, had decided to visit Jimmy before he saw anyone else.

Luke wasn't truly angry with Jimmy, even though his actions may have led to Luke's final break with the Cygnets, but he did want to make it clear that he felt betrayed by the boy's actions and that what happened to Press was not only inexcusable but dangerous. Press might have been killed. But somewhere along his way, Luke's irritation calmed and he understood that Jimmy hadn't acted knowingly or maliciously; on the contrary, his actions were the result of animal instincts, which neither he nor any of the others understood very well, as far as he could tell from their behavior both as animals and humans. And this could have been the problem that Ms. Royce was trying to explain to him – one's animal nature could easily take control of one's human nature if one was not careful. Of course, he didn't know why Ms. Royce would have suggested such a thing unless she herself was an animal, but that was impossible and so she might have made a good guess at Luke's feelings or Luke may have misunderstood what she said or was trying to say. It didn't matter either way, because it was clear from what had happened that one had to be careful when going about as an animal, and being an animal didn't exactly appeal to Luke at the moment. He wanted to put that business aside for now, maybe even forever. Luke had arrived at Jimmy's front steps just as Jimmy stepped out of the house and closed the door behind him.

"I'm going for a walk," Jimmy said, looking at Luke as if he was the last person he expected to show up. Luke nodded without saying a word, and the two of them began walking down the sidewalk in the direction of the park, which was several blocks away.

Neither one of them said a word for at least five minutes, but their minds were filled with thoughts about what had happened and what the other boy was thinking about it. Jimmy was the first to break the silence. "I hope Press is okay," he said, without looking at Luke or slackening his pace.

"She's okay, I think," Luke replied, "although her arm was hurt. There wasn't much blood, so I'm sure it's minor. Sometimes Press can be a little dramatic."

"Okay. But you don't think she's going to say anything, do you?" Jimmy glanced at Luke when he said this, and, while he was waiting for an answer, he continued to look at Luke out the corner of his eyes.

Luke was a little put off by Jimmy's seeming callousness ('The last thing anyone should be worried about is whether Press is going to tell anyone,' he reflected), although he decided that Jimmy wasn't really a mean or unfeeling person, only someone who had confronted his own animal nature and had found the experience unsettling. Luke felt the same way. But while he was troubled by the degree to which Jimmy's non-human nature had taken control of his judgment, Luke was determined not to behave like Iowa and the Cygnets, tossing aside friends for no reason at all. He was better than that – he was better than them -- and, besides, he actually liked Jimmy.

"No, of course not. She's not like that."

"But what if she does?" Jimmy had stopped and was looking right at Luke.

"I don't know. She's not going to say anything. Isn't that enough?"

They continued on in silence until they reached an open field about a quarter mile away. The field wasn't connected to the park, and as far as fields go it was pretty barren, little more than a few grassy hills, numerous small bushes, and some stunted trees. There was no lake; but a little stream crawled its way through the field on its way to the lake where Iowa and the others were sure to be.

Once they entered the field and were far enough away from the houses, Jimmy quickly changed into a dog. Luke hesitated, but seeing Jimmy bouncing around at his feet and recalling the way the Cygnets had treated him, he followed suit and changed into a dog. Luke felt a little guilty doing something that he was certain he would never again do, but as soon as he stood up and stretched his legs, guilt was the farthest thing from his mind – indeed, he felt excited, and he blamed the Cygnets for trying to prevent him from experiencing the very thing that they themselves indulged in. 'It's just like them,' he thought in a vague, nearly wordless way.

There was something about being a dog that suited Luke's sensitivities. For one thing, he didn't like the water so much. The lake was beautiful, especially at the end of day when the sun's dying light covered the surface of the water with gold and ruby tones. But he didn't want to sit in it all day. Then again, swans had never interested him, because they can't move quickly and were forced to swim to the center of the lake whenever danger approached. If that weren't enough, the swans were confined to the lake unless they changed back to human form, and they couldn't go to another body of water unless there were other swans there, otherwise they could attract a lot of unwanted attention ('Imagine seeing a swan in the neighborhood swimming pool,' he told himself). Luke was indeed sorry that Press had been injured, but he hadn't touched her and, besides, she should have anticipated some of the dangers when she chose to be a swan.

A dog, on the other hand, is an extraordinary creature, possibly more amazing than even a human being. In the first place, it possesses speed and cunning, enabling it to go almost anywhere without being seen or at least without attracting undo attention. In the second place, a dog can live off the land without training or struggling. This means that a dog can go where it wants, when it wants, and it doesn't have to worry about its next meal or where it is going to spend the night. In the third place…well, the third place doesn't matter. What does matter is the fact that dogs are loyal, unfailingly so, unlike stupid birds, which are bound to turn against someone sooner or later, generally sooner. For a brief second, Luke remembered Iowa, and he felt sorry for her because the swans would eventually turn against her as they turned against him, but this feeling quickly faded as he contemplated the joys of being a wonderful, majestic – and loyal – animal, congratulating himself on having made the right choice. There was nothing better than being a dog, or being with a dog, and he wished that he still had his dog and that the two of them could enjoy this blissful state together, and forever.

Luke and Jimmy spent the rest of the day charging across the field, leaping over hills and holes, wrestling and biting one another on the neck (gently, of course, since this was play), and sometimes chasing squirrels and other small animals. Actually,

Luke didn't chase the animals as much as he followed Jimmy, who loved to chase anything that moved, especially the large rabbit that he must have chased for over a mile until he, nearly exhausted, was forced to give up when the rabbit jumped down a water drain and disappeared from sight. Jimmy never got within more than six inches of the rabbit, but that was enough to stir his instincts and he continued hectoring the poor animal. Luke did his best to keep up, but after a while it became clear that he could hang back and wait for Jimmy and the rabbit to cross and re-cross his path and take a rather leisurely approach to keeping his eyes on Jimmy. Unfortunately for Jimmy, he got tangled in a mess of sharp sticks and needles, but since these apparently itched more than hurt (shortly after the chase, Jimmy scratched himself furiously and tugged at the larger pieces with his teeth), Luke couldn't exactly feel sorry for Jimmy. He was thankful, however, that he didn't have the same trouble.

Late in the afternoon, as the sun was setting and the field was growing dim, Luke and Jimmy began to feel the pain of hunger and longed to be in bed at rest. Walking on the sidewalk on their way home, Jimmy suddenly darted across the street and was nearly struck by a car. The car's tires squealed, and the bumper of the car had missed him by inches, if that. He had seen something on the other side of the street, and without giving a single thought to anything else immediately charged off to see what it was. It was a squirrel, and Jimmy easily dispatched it, after which he dropped it in the gutter. Trotting back to Luke as if nothing had happened, the two continued on to Jimmy's house, where they both changed back to humans and returned to their respective houses.

In his bedroom after dinner, Luke laid on his stomach across his bed, from the top corner to the opposite bottom corner, his chin held up by his fists stacked on top of each other and, in the dim light (he had only turned on a dim lamp at his desk), he thought about everything that had happened this day. He vividly recalled running through the tall grass and jumping over ditches that would have been impossible to surmount as a human. But as a dog, these things seemed easy, and his speed was far beyond anything he had ever experienced. True, he had gone much faster in a car, but he had never propelled himself with such speed and agility before – he could run like lightning and then turn abruptly, and continue on leaping over hills and holes hardly without tiring. He did get a little tired from time to time, and he always needed water, but a short break was enough to reenergize him and, of course, he could drink from the stream, the gutter, or practically wherever he felt like.

Luke loved how his shoulders felt when he was a dog. They didn't feel massive, not like a weightlifter's, but they did feel strong and, again, agile. His hind legs, however, were simply amazing. Pushing off with his hind legs, he could move quickly, propelling himself up the steepest hill or across the slipperiest ravine without the least bit of effort; he could even force himself upward and onto a rock or ridge easily, even if it were three times his height. He also loved how he could move his skin and muscles in ways that he couldn't have imagined as a human (how could a human imagine wagging a rail unless he had firsthand experience?). But most amazing of all were his heightened senses. Luke could perceive sounds that he had never heard before, sounds that he didn't know existed before becoming a dog. Take, for example, a yellow tulip. To most human ears, it doesn't make a sound even when its petals were rustled, but as Luke discovered, a tulip can be a noisy neighbor, either producing a wet, sticky groan as it reaches slowly out of the ground, or a syrupy swish when it is moved, perhaps touched by the wind or by the smooth, slender chest of a deer, pushing it aside to reach a blueberry or a blood-red strawberry. Luke could also hear faint tunes as they floated through the air currents overhead, especially at night, music that described the shape, mass, and location of some object. He couldn't always identify what exactly made the music, but from the timbre he could visualize the number of legs the object had, whether or not it had fur and the length of the fur, and if by chance it was moving in his direction, even if it was still a couple of miles away. Similarly, Luke found that he could distinguish one person from another, one dog from another, by the way they smelled or, to be precise, by the way the accumulation of their bodily scents (the right ear emitted a different smell than the left leg) differentiated one individual from another. The various pieces created a distinct and unmistakable whole, enabling Luke the dog to stick his nose into the air and, after locating the right air current, distinguish an anonymous little boy stealing raspberries while his mother, chatting on her phone, looked in the opposite direction, even though the bush, the boy, and his mother were out of sight and some distance away.

Luke was convinced that he no longer needed his toys and other objects to have fun or fill his day with peace and happiness, not while he could change into a dog any moment and live a life more vivid than any he could ever have dreamed of. Luke turned over on his side and rested his head on his right fist. 'I don't know why I have to stay here,' he told himself, 'not when I could be out and doing whatever I wanted. Who can stop me?' Luke abruptly stood up and, listening to see if his parents were in bed, he walked quietly over to his window, lifted it, and slipped out of the house.

Chapter Twenty-Five - He could see a faint mist rising

The air was cool – he could see a faint mist rising from the tip of his nose – but he felt as warm and comfortable as he had been in the house. He shook his body from nose to tail, after which he stretched each leg, sticking his back legs out first and then his front legs. Eager to explore the neighborhood, Luke trotted around the house, jumping over a coiled hose, and bounded into the front yard, where he suddenly paused. Turning his head this way and that, he listened carefully for signs that anyone was stirring in his house (no lights were on) or somewhere nearby, a neighbor, for example, or someone else he might know. When it was clear that he was alone, he trotted out of the yard and meandered up one block and down another until, by accident, he found himself within yards of Jimmy's house. It was obvious that everyone was asleep in that house, too, because the lights were out and area surrounding the house was just as quiet as it had been at his own house. Luke was about to turn and head in another direction when he scented Jimmy's presence on the sidewalk. It was only one spot, which indicated that he had come out of his house, crossed the street, and like Luke was going somewhere in the night. Buoyed by the scent, Luke decided to follow Jimmy's trail and, once he located him, spend the rest of the evening with him.

Actually, Jimmy's trail amused him. The dog didn't follow a straight line, or even take the most direct route to wherever he was going, although Luke could tell that he was moving with some degree of urgency. Jimmy meandered from one side of the road or walk to the other, turning one corner after another, going round a block, going up a small hill and then back down the very side he just climbed, and stopping, over and over, to relieve himself. Some of it made sense to Luke, but the desire to go to a particular place at night, and the need to get there fairly quickly, seemed to contradict Jimmy's wanderings, or else Jimmy behaved in a way that contradicted the urgency Luke sensed in Jimmy. Luke persevered, however, and an hour later he arrived at the entrance of the park, the very place where he used to meet Press, Lu, Dana, and of course Iowa.

Luke hesitated. For a few seconds, images of the Cygnets flashed through his mind, and he could see as clearly as day many of the wonderful times they had together, although as he watched the memories the names of the individual Cygnets dissolved from his memory. He tried to recall the names, but it was no use; nothing would come back. Still, he was certain that these had been good times, maybe even great times, and yet after a while they, too, began to fade, each one disappearing like powdered chocolate in a glass of milk, and he began to sense something sad or unfortunate behind the images, even though he couldn't recall a single one that hadn't been happy. Because of the underlying sadness, which in some cases lingered on after the dissolution of the memory, Luke couldn't help wondering if entering the park was a mistake and, as he rolled it around in his mind, if he should turn around and see Jimmy some other night. Unlike his friend, Luke didn't feel any particular urgency to enter the park; besides, there were plenty of other places to go that were fun and, hopefully, not associated with anything troubling or disturbing. Running up and down the streets, for example, was more than enough fun for any night, especially after everyone was in bed and didn't care whether you were in their yard, garden, or trash can.

Luke started to turn around – he decided that he could meet Jimmy some other night -- when the memories suddenly increased, and he recalled the time before the Cygnets became animals, when Lu won a game of sticks and had to be persuaded that she and not Dana had been victorious, when they all sat together at the water's edge on a warm summer evening and watched the stars crossing the evening sky, when they talked about everything under the sun -- school, friends, parents, and anything else that came to mind – and when they were all friends and none of them would have said an unkind word to him, much less turned against him. Extraordinarily vivid memories filled his mind, and for a few seconds he was back with the Cygnets, playing, swimming, and simply enjoying the time he spent with them. But no sooner had he turned to spend the evening some other place than something happened -- all the memories that had been crowding his mind suddenly vanished, disappearing as quickly and irrevocably as though someone had pulled their plug, and he was left wondering why he had hesitated and if he still had time to catch up with Jimmy.

Once in the park, Luke followed Jimmy along the very path that he and the Cygnets had used for years, only this time it meant nothing to him – it aroused no memories or second thoughts about what he was doing – and, in fact, he was pleased, because it allowed him to avoid the bushes and thorns around the trees, which stuck to his fur and, after a while, managed to burrow their way to his skin, where they poked and prodded his sensitive flesh. After a couple of minutes – less than half the time it took to jog it by human foot – he arrived at the clearing by the lake. There was a moment here, as well, too brief to be measured, in which something flashed in his mind (a memory or a warning, he couldn't tell which), but since it neither lingered nor recurred, Luke didn't think another thing about it and, instead, focused his attention on everything before him: the black, undulating surface of the water; the moon's bright light, which spread across the water like a single sidewalk of light; the faint stars in the sky, which brightened the night sky and outlined the trees and grasses surrounding him and the lake; and the dark shadows everywhere, which obscured the individual trees, bushes, and the long stalks of grass close to the water.

While he looked out across the grass and the shadows expecting to find Jimmy, who was somewhere nearby (Luke could both hear and smell his presence), Luke noticed several sets of glistening lights floating in the shadows, lights that he now knew were the eyes of other dogs. Looking at the eyes, sniffing the air to locate Jimmy – who, it turned out, was only a few feet away – Luke felt surprisingly comfortable, as if he was among a large group of like-minded beings, a group of animals just like himself. He was pleased to be among his own kind, experiencing a kinship that could not be severed because of the unhappiness of one or more individuals. Catching sight of Jimmy out the corner of his eye (Jimmy was about ten feet away and standing expectantly a few inches from the edge of the water), Luke trotted over to him and nuzzled him under his hairy chin and against the side of his muzzle, his thick whiskers tickling his own. He felt at home, as if he was always meant to be there. Jimmy, however, didn't budge and kept his nose angled at something on the other side of the lake.

Jimmy was focused on something deep in the shadows on the other side of the lake. Luke glanced in the same direction, but not seeing anything he turned back to Jimmy and, for some reason, looked out to the bright eyes penetrating the darkness behind Jimmy. They, too, were looking in the same direction, no doubt fixated on the very same object that captured Jimmy's attention. Curious, Luke turned back to Jimmy and then to the water to see what they were all trying to see, and he still couldn't see anything but a massive wall of darkness. He could hear cackles, screeches, groans, and chirps, but the sounds were obviously coming from the woods and not associated with anything that Jimmy and the rest of the dogs were preoccupied with. Luke was about to ask Jimmy what was so interesting about the shadows (three short barks would have done it), when he began to sense the presence of something substantial – and familiar – at the other end of the lake. There was a peculiar hay-like smell emanating from the area and, as he lifted his nose to home in on the smell, he could feel strange undulations on the surface of the water and a mild ruffling of the air in the same location, and he couldn't help thinking that something in the darkness was coming his way, something alive. There were other sensations, too – a faint hush, a high-pitched click, and, suddenly, a soft clap that increased the undulations and disturbances – which, combined with everything else, told him that there were large animals in the water, birds, possibly swans.

Neither the presence of the birds nor the dogs' strange obsession with the birds suggested that something was wrong or not quite right. On the contrary, the tension and excitement that he sensed in Jimmy and the other dogs raised his own level of anticipation and excitement, even though at this moment he didn't quite share their near frenzied desire to act aggressively. Luke wasn't concerned about the birds, since the earlier memories were now gone and there was nothing to connect the birds to events in his past, and yet he wasn't interested in doing the kinds of things that he knew Jimmy and the dogs wanted to do – dispatching animals or hectoring them to the point of death. It just didn't seem interesting, especially now when something again floated into the back of his mind, telling him to leave the park. It was little more than a vague uneasiness, the kind of sensation that is easy to discount because it offers little in the way of justification. But even if Luke were interested in what he suspected that the dogs were planning to do, he wasn't interested in waiting until they got the opportunity or, for that matter, competing with the others for some small piece of the entertainment, which he knew would invariably be the case. Luke loved the other dogs, but for some reason he was no longer eager or interested to do the things that they wanted to do and, instead, wanted to play with Jimmy exclusively, someplace where the others couldn't intrude.

Luke muzzled Jimmy again to see if he wanted to run around in another field or leave the park altogether, but Jimmy didn't budge and in response to a second nudge, he abruptly turned to Luke and grabbed the back of his neck with his powerful canines. Luke wasn't hurt, but he also didn't have the strength to throw him off. When Jimmy released him, accompanying the release with a deep growl, Luke backed away and then trotted a good fifteen or twenty feet away from Jimmy and the others.

Luke watched Jimmy for a few more minutes until he realized that he was wasting his time. Jimmy wasn't going to change his mind and play with Luke, certainly not this evening. Luke shook himself and glanced at the eyes and then at the lake. He liked Jimmy, although he really couldn't say why, since they had so few things in common. Jimmy did enjoy running back and forth and testing his physical agility, which is really what Luke wanted to do this night, but Jimmy also liked killing things, especially squirrels, rabbits, cats, and other small animals. That was clear not only by the numbers of animals he killed, but also by the manner in which he would pounce and sink his long canines into their flesh, relishing the way his teeth penetrated the skin and crushed the bones. But this didn't interest Luke. It didn't bother him – the killing of another animal was a matter of indifference to him as it is with all dogs – but, at the same time, it didn't particularly appeal to him, either. The chase was more fun than the kill, especially when it required him to exercise his muscles and physical capabilities to their limits. But just as Luke began trotting back to the woods (he had decided to go home, since he was becoming tired and nothing at that moment seemed especially interesting to explore), something inside urged him to stop and take one more look at Jimmy.

Turning and looking at his friend, Luke noticed that Jimmy was starting to behave erratically -- he was pacing back and forth at the water's edge and, pausing from time to time to sniff the air, whimpering slightly over something that he desperately wanted to do. Luke knew immediately what was on Jimmy's mind and the cause of his whimpering, but, once again, this sort of thing didn't interest Luke and, even less interesting at the moment, was watching Jimmy do it. The birds were like any other animals, and Luke couldn't understand why Jimmy was so insistent – no, on edge with excitement – on killing these birds. Maybe they were fun to kill, but to attack them now while they were still on the water seemed like a lot of work for a small amount of fun. While Luke was mulling this over in his mind, it also occurred to him that a few swans were not enough to sate the nervous energy of the dogs (without seeing them, he could feel their tension), and when they turned for something else to calm their nerves, he didn't want that something else to be him.

Not waiting to find out for sure, Luke headed toward the path and galloped into the woods. He didn't stop once he was out of sight of the lake and the dogs, but continued on toward home at a quick, albeit comfortable, pace. All was well. He had heard frenzied barking a few moments earlier – probably a sign that one or more of the swans had been dispatched – but he wasn't going to return to the lake to check it out and, besides, he now wanted more than anything to go home and roll up onto the rug next to his bed. It was a wonderful rug. It had been made from thick twines of yarn as big as one's fingers, and it was so heavy that one could roll on it without sending the rug sliding under the bed. It was just the perfect thing to ease one's tired bones.

Thinking about the rug, his home, and sleeping – maybe for an entire day – Luke happily rounded a sharp corner on the path, which led to a narrow passageway before reaching the open areas near the edge of the park, and came to an abrupt halt, his feet skidding on the dirt and his tail and rear legs nearly forced to the ground. Directly in front of him, not more than fifteen feet away, was a gigantic, brownish-black shadow that seemed to be straddling the entire width of the path, blocking Luke's exit from the park.

Luke had never seen anything like it, certainly not in the park, and as he stared at the strange, mountainous shape with amazement, he was perplexed by the stale, musty smell emanating from various parts of its body. For a moment or two, as he eyed this unmoving object, Luke wondered if it was some kind of deer. The animal looked somewhat like a deer, although its hide was rough and shaggy, its shoulders high and rounded, and it had a peculiar, furry wattle beneath its square jaw. The animal was also larger and more muscular than any deer he had encountered in the park (or anywhere else, for that matter) – roughly three times the size of the largest deer he had ever seen – and it sported spiked, oar-like antlers that were bigger than he or Jimmy were. But if it were a deer, it certainly didn't behave like other deer, which flee the second they encounter another animal. This one didn't budge at the sight of Luke. In fact, the tense, sinewy muscles in its legs and neck, the manner in which it locked its cold, black eyes onto Luke's, and the way the nostrils of its massive snout expanded and contracted, inhaling and exhaling moist, steamy air, strongly suggested that whatever kind of animal this was, it wasn't daunted by the sudden appearance of Luke.

Luke's initial reaction to the unexpected appearance of the strange creature was to bark loudly and continuously, which was his way of warning the animal to stay back and a demonstration that he, Luke, was not afraid of it, whatever it was. Luke also hoped that, after a few moments of raucous barking interspersed with growling and biting gestures, his own aggressive behavior would throw the animal off guard and force it to step aside to allow Luke through. Unfortunately, the animal didn't budge; and since it occupied the entire width of the path, which at that point was bound on either side with large boulders and massive trees, Luke realized that he would have to turn around and find another exit from the park. Since there was no convenient way of getting around the rocks, trees, and dense bush, he decided that it would be easiest to exit the park from the other side of the lake, which meant that he would again have to encounter Jimmy and his friends. At the moment, this seemed preferable to confronting the animal, which neither blinked nor batted an ear at Luke's presence and the racket he was making. But weren't all animals afraid of a barking dog?

Slowly and carefully backing away (Luke didn't want to spook the animal), while constantly barking warnings for the animal to keep its distance, Luke added another ten feet or so of space between him and the animal before he was ready to turn around and retreat to the lake. Confident now that he was beyond the reach of the animal, Luke turned around only to be confronted by two more gigantic beasts, standing side by side, shoulder pressed against shoulder, both looking like the first and as seemingly unmovable, blocking his exit. Unfortunately, the path at this point was little more than a narrow tunnel bound by densely packed trees and thick bushes with sharp nettles up and down their stalks and branches, which prevented his exit as effectively as the rock walls had done on the other side of the path. In fact, there was less space between these beasts – together, they seemed almost as solid and impermeable as one of the boulders next to the path – than the other, making Luke shudder and wonder how he was going to escape the park and these strange…things.

Jumping back and bounding several steps back toward the first beast until he was about halfway between the first animal and the other two, Luke stood sideways to the animals and glanced back and forth to keep an eye on them and ensure that if any of them were to move, he would have sufficient time to react. Naturally, he couldn't fathom how he would react (he had never faced a situation even vaguely resembling this one), but he didn't want to be caught off guard and wanted at least the opportunity to respond. Indeed, there was nowhere to hide if one or all of them charged, and, even though he was confident he could dodge a few thrusts of the animals' gigantic antlers, he wasn't entirely certain how long he could stay out of their reach if they coordinated their efforts. Moving his eyes anxiously back and forth while the animals stared at him, occasionally blowing snot out their noses and licking their square jaws, Luke tried to fathom which animal was going to move first and which would give him the opening he needed to save his life. Each one kept its place for several minutes before Luke caught sight of the two animals slowly lowering their heads in unison, as if they were a single being, and positioning their antlers so that they appeared to be a solid, impenetrable wall. Knowing that he couldn't stand motionless for much longer, Luke tried to think of something that would enable him to escape, although the only things that came immediately to mind were his home and the thick rug on his floor. Luke shook himself from his head to his tail to clear his mind and sharpen his senses, after which he glanced at the animals on both sides to assess his chances. Clearly, there were no good choices, but it seemed easier to get by one animal as long as he found a way of diverting its attention or maybe even making it back away (most animals are afraid of dogs, he told himself again).

Luke turned to face the solitary animal, the largest deer-like creature he had ever seen, which suddenly seemed to be coming alive as if it had been asleep when he first encountered it. Mesmerized, he took a half-step back and stared at the animal, which shook its shaggy head and gigantic antlers while snorting and expelling large plumes of sour-smelling steam and snot as if it were getting ready for some tremendous action. Its black, lifeless eyes locked onto Luke, and like a bull it pawed the ground twice with its right hoof, while the muscles in its shoulders, legs, and haunches tightened like a cat's muscles tighten just before attacking its prey. While he tried to figure out his response to the animal in front of him, Luke nevertheless kept a wary ear open for signs that the animals behind him were beginning to stir and come his way. How could one be in a more troublesome situation? Luckily, the animals behind him seemed to be content, or at least they didn't seem to be angry or determined to do anything, unlike the animal facing him, and Luke felt certain that it would be only a matter of minutes, maybe seconds, before he would have to deal with the much larger animal. He tried to come up with something, but before he could formulate a single idea that would either defuse its rising anger or enable him to escape and leave the park, the animal stabbed his antlers into the dirt and, jerking its head violently to one side, scooped up a mass of dirt and weeds from the path and, with a sharp, upward movement of its head, threw it at Luke, striking him on the nose of the left side of his head. Luke flinched and involuntarily crouched, his ears lowered and his tail flush against his hind leg.

Luke was unhurt, despite the amount of dirt and rocks that hit his face, and while he waited for the animal to follow this action with another, he straightened himself, shook his head and shoulders, and then carefully turned again toward the animal. Luke was surprised when he again looked at the deer or whatever it was, for its aggression seemed to have dissipated (the muscles and tendons in its body appeared to have slackened), as if that one violent action had cost it so much energy that it needed to relax before it could undertake another violent action, and it was now eyeing Luke as before, malevolently but apparently not with the intent of attacking any time soon. The thought that he still had a few minutes left to come up with something to get him out of this predicament somehow replenished both his spirits and his mental capabilities, and he started to moot about several possible ways to get around the animal while keeping himself from getting hurt.

Since the animal had still not budged from the center of the path, it occurred to Luke that his best chance of avoiding the animal (that is, getting around it unscathed) was either to move it to one side so that he could squeeze by it or, which was extremely risky, to scramble underneath it (there was plenty of room beneath the animal, unless it lowered its antlers, and Luke was positive that the animal was not quick enough to respond once he had reached its belly). Because of the current calm, Luke was not yet desperate enough to try making his way under the animal, and so he began to consider various means of getting the animal to move to one side or the other, out of the center of the path where it blocked his exit as effectively as the other two animals standing side by side. Of all the possibilities he considered, only one seemed reasonable enough to work and keep him from being maimed or killed. It was simple. He would show the animal that he wasn't afraid of it and that he was preparing to attack it from one side or the other. The animal would naturally respond and, moving to one side or the other, open up a space wide enough for Luke to slip through and escape.

Hopeful that this was a good plan, Luke tightened his shoulders, exposed his teeth (especially his large canines) and, growling loudly, cautiously took five or six steps toward the left side of the animal, hoping that it would move in the same lateral direction and inadvertently open a reasonably-sized space. And, indeed, for a few seconds, it seemed to work. As Luke continued inching toward the animal, it adjusted its bulk and seemed to be preparing for a suicidal attack from Luke. Unfortunately, the animal either didn't understand Luke's plan or had something else in mind when it moved, because it suddenly snorted loudly and violently, took two swift steps toward Luke and angled its antlers – antlers which now seemed larger than any normal-sized deer –

directly at him. Luke still wasn't certain what the animal had in mind, despite the formidable array of sharp spikes aimed directly at him, and so he moved another couple of steps toward it to signal both his intentions and his lack of fear, which the deer countered by moving another three or four steps toward Luke, putting it only a few feet from Luke.

With the animal so close that he could feel its hot breath, Luke carefully angled his body so that he could spring forward and pivot around the animal's right flank before it realized what had happened. The animal, however, seemed to read Luke's mind, for it shifted its weight to block any possible move in that direction and, again, angled its antlers down toward Luke as if was about ready to charge. Luke was confident that he was quicker and more agile than the much larger animal, and so he immediately turned and, pushing off as hard as he could with his hind legs, hurled himself toward the other side of the animal, hoping to catch the animal off guard. Surprisingly, it proved more nimble than he had anticipated and, turning, blocked Luke's escape.

Once again, Luke and the deer faced one another. Knowing now that it was going to be difficult to get around the animal, Luke decided to take the matter head on. Growling loudly and barking several times, he charged, hoping that his own audacity would either force the animal to retreat or would surprise it so that it would stand still, its head high enough off the ground to enable Luke to squeeze underneath it and run out of the park. But, again, the animal seemed to know what Luke had in mind, for it charged Luke with lightning speed and, positioning its antlers toward the ground like a bull dozer, managed to collect Luke in a single movement and send him tumbling into the air. Falling on his side, Luke felt his left leg bend unnaturally and painfully; it wasn't broken, though, because he was able to pick himself up and quickly back away from the animal, limping as he did so. But before Luke had a chance to regain all his senses and take another step, the much larger animal again charged, and this time it scooped up Luke in its massive antlers and, after throwing him to the ground, pinned him to the dirt with its antlers, which were like a giant cage.

Luke didn't know what was happening. For a few seconds, he felt as if he were floating in a gray, featureless cloud, after which he began to see vague shadows and hear peculiar, muffled sounds, noises that were unlike anything he had ever heard before. But as his mind began to clear, he began to hear a faint, yelping sound, which gradually became louder and louder, the volume increasing with the improving clarity of his vision, until he realized that the sound was his own yelping because the animal was holding him to the ground and preventing him from making all but the slightest movements. The animal, however, wasn't moved by Luke's pain, and it continued to keep him face down on the ground while it snorted madly, loudly, as if every sound Luke made – as if his very existence – infuriated it.

Engulfed by the hot, acrid breath of the animal, Luke started to feel sick to his stomach and he might have vomited had he not noticed a change that took his mind off of everything else. The massive force of the animal on top of him started to shift, putting more weight on his legs and stomach and forcing him forward, back first, along the path in the opposite direction of the entrance. Luke couldn't move anything except his eyes, but he could feel the dirt piling up against his back, as if his back were the blade of the bulldozer, and he could feel each rock and stick that didn't move tear through his fur and force his bones deeper into his body. Because of his inability to resist, the human side of him gradually floated to the surface of his consciousness and he began to see that his life, like the lives of the swans, was coming to a premature end, and for only the second time since becoming a dog, Luke not only regretted his choice but wished that he had never made the choice at all. He didn't want to be an animal anymore, and he prayed to something that if the unrelenting deer would only relent, if it would release the pressure on him just enough to allow him to escape, he would change to human form and never again change into a dog – never again desire to be anything other than his true self, a human being named Luke.

Having uttered his prayer, Luke noticed that his forward momentum was beginning to slow and, for the briefest moment, he started to believe that the animal would release him and that he would be able to keep his promise. But as it turned out, the animal was not slowing at all. Luke's body was stuck against a large rock or some other obstruction and, instead of moving with the antlers, his back began to twist and bend, his legs press into his body, and

223

his pain increased to such a point that he was positive that his back would shatter at any second. The unnatural contortions of his body were also twisting his head upward and, for a second, he thought he caught a glimpse of the animal's lifeless, remorseless eyes. It was the end, and Luke closed his eyes so that he didn't have to witness it.

Suddenly, the pressure ceased, his back, neck, and head returned to a more natural position, and for some reason the animal took a step back, releasing Luke. But did it release him? Perhaps it was only playing with him, like Jimmy was probably playing with the swans, and any second it would charge again and finish him off. Indeed, it would be easy, for while Luke may not have been hurt as badly as it seemed, he was wobbly as he stood up and nearly fell over when he tried to shake himself. Looking up at the animal, which towered above him like a mountain, Luke prepared for the worst, this time with his eyes open, but just when it seemed ready to finish him off, something happened. Its shape and texture began to blur and become indistinct, its dull brown color started to fade into an indistinct gray, after which it fell to the ground like a pile of leaves blowing by a gentle wind. Luke couldn't believe his eyes, but before he had had a chance to question them, the leaves became a human, and that human was Ms. Royce.

Chapter Twenty-Six - With an expression that matched the deer's

Ms. Royce faced Luke with an expression that matched the deer's. Luke, too, changed to human form and stood facing Ms. Royce, but with none of the strength and exuberance he had had as a dog. In fact, in the brief seconds before he understood what had just happened, he nearly fell down at the sight of Ms. Royce. Once he gathered his senses, though, her appearance seemed almost as natural and expected as it would have on the school campus.

"Why did you do it?" she demanded. "Don't you have any sense? Do you realize what's going to happen now because of you?"

"Me?" Luke cried, not knowing what it was he could have done. It occurred to him, however, that Press and the others had spoken to her about what Jimmy had done to Press and that she was not only holding him responsible for that but also for what Jimmy may have done since then. "I didn't do anything. I didn't hurt Press or anyone else. It was Jimmy. It was Jimmy."

"No, it wasn't Jimmy. It was you. You should have had more sense and, because of you, others are going to be hurt."

"No, no, I made mistakes, but Jimmy hurt Press, not me. I was mad at her, I almost wanted to hurt her myself, but I didn't lay a hand on her arm, wing, or whatever. Please, you have to believe me. Ask Iowa. She was there. She won't lie." He hesitated slightly having said that, because he wasn't sure that Iowa was alive to say anything. Still, he thought it best at the moment not to go into too much detail.

Ms. Royce stared at Luke and, crossing her arms, she shook her head slightly. "I know you didn't hurt Press. And I don't need to hear that from Iowa or anyone else. You wouldn't do anything like that. She was your friend, despite your problems."

"Then why is everyone mad at me?"

"Because you showed Jimmy how to change. You knew that he had a mean streak in him, and yet you showed him how to do it and awakened a wild animal in our midst."

"He was practically the only friend I had. The others…you don't understand."

"I understand more than you think. Whatever was going on between you and the others is no excuse for what you did. Do you understand me? You made a serious mistake showing Jimmy how to change. You compounded this mistake by giving him the power to show others. Do you have any idea how many people he's told? Do you have any idea how many uncontrollable animals are potentially roaming our streets? Do you understand what I'm trying to tell you? I'm not sure I can put the genie back into the…"

Recognizing the truth of Ms. Royce's words, Luke dropped to the ground and, sitting in the soft dirt of the path, he covered his eyes with both hands and began to cry. "I'm sorry, I'm sorry," he moaned. "Please, forgive me."

Ms. Royce hesitated for a moment. "Get up," she said, without a trace of sympathy in her voice. "Get up. You are going to help us solve this problem."

Luke slowly stood up (he was still a little wobbly) and, while he faced Ms. Royce, he couldn't look at her. He let his chin fall to his chest while he waited for what would happen next.

"Look at me," Ms. Royce commanded. "Remember, it's your turn to help me. It is your only chance. Do you understand me? Good. Unless you're not serious, I want you to turn around and follow me to the lake."

Luke looked into her face and practically wilted before her stern expression. He had never seen her so serious, and she radiated so much power – and authority – that he was willing to do practically anything to change her expression, to bring back the old Ms. Royce. He was ready to follow her without question when she turned and faced the direction of the lake. But before they had taken two steps, she abruptly took a quick step to the side, off the path, leaving Luke alone on the path and facing all the strange, foreboding creatures that were now clustered around him, eyeing him, blocking his way.

A full moon was now directly overhead, unobstructed by trees or dark clouds, and its pale, grayish light illuminated the path and dispersed many of the shadows among the surrounding trees and rocks. Luke could clearly see several large deer, just like Ms.

Royce standing directly in front of him, not more than ten feet away, antlers poised for action. Next to them, on Luke's right, were two great, brown bears, whose heads twisted back and forth and whose mouths were hanging open ready to attack. Large wolves, three or four, stood next to the bears, one of which was baring its teeth and growling quietly. After this, there were foxes, deer, and an assortment of other animals either next to the large animals or standing directly underneath them. On the other side of the deer blocking the way were horses, leopards, and even more deer. Perhaps because of his experience with Ms. Royce, Luke shuddered when he looked at them, especially when they jostled together to get a good look at him, their antlers making clicking and clacking sounds as they banged against one another.

Luke took a half-step back. He stared at the emotionless faces of the animals and at their cold, lifeless eyes, and he couldn't help wondering how such massive animals as these got to this point without making a sound or causing a stir because of their smell (in fact, the movement of these animals either along the path or through the woods should have rattled the woods and raised alarms among the humans outside of the park) and, more importantly, he was concerned about what they were going to do now that they had seen him. Ms. Royce, however, sensed Luke's quandary and grabbed his left arm and pulled him off the path. That seemed to be the signal for the animals to step onto the path and apparently head for the lake, each one of them craning his head and glancing at Luke as they passed by, making Luke feel like a general reviewing his troops as they paraded past him on their way to war.

"This is no time to be afraid," Ms. Royce said, as the thuds of their hooves reverberated from the ground and echoed among the trees. "We are all the same, except that we didn't come into being out of selfishness and stupidity. We all made conscious, careful decisions, since we were mature and understood the gravity of having such a choice. We chose wisely, for the most part, because we were willing – we are willing – to take responsibility for our actions. Does this make sense to you?" She stood next to Luke, just to the side of the path, but instead of looking at Luke, she watched the passing parade and, from time to time, nodded at certain animals as they passed by.

Luke nodded, knowing that Ms. Royce didn't need to hear his answer to know whether or not he agreed with her. "But who are they?" Luke whispered, fearing to disturb either the animals or the trees. A large crow cawed several times overhead and then floated down and landed on the back of a passing bear. As the bear sauntered by Luke, both animals stared at him as if they knew him, or at least as if they held him responsible for their presence this evening.

"Who are they? How can you be so shortsighted? They are the people who live here, in the town, or at least a lot of them are. Do you see that wolf?" she asked, as a thin timber wolf walked along the edge of the path, glancing nervously from one side to the other. "That's our school superintendent, a really remarkable man." The wolf paused before disappearing into the woods and, glancing back at Ms. Royce, cocked his head as if he were about to howl. "None of that, Tom," Ms. Royce said, addressing him in a friendly, bantering tone. "We have enough problems right now, and we don't want to compound them by announcing our presence to the whole world." He shook his head and trotted out of sight.

"He's normally very careful," she added. "Now, do you see that horse? That's Mr. Ralston, our new gym teacher. He came to us from out of state and…well, it's interesting that he's one of us, isn't it? Do you see those foxes? Those are your neighbors from across the street. They were also friendly with Iowa's mother, although I don't think they thought too highly of her father. But they like your family quite a bit." For several minutes after that, she continued to point out people -- or rather animals that were people, too – whom Luke knew quite well, or well enough to speak to when he saw them on the street, at the mall, in the stores, or even in their homes, his parents being quite friendly with many of the persons Ms. Royce mentioned.

"I…I," Luke tried to speak coherently, but he kept stumbling over his words because everything around him was startling and, in many ways, incomprehensible. "I…or are…is everyone one in the city an…animal, too? My parents, where are they?"

"I've pointed out the people so that you would understand what a correct choice looks like. It's none of your business who is or who isn't, and as far as your parents are concerned, only they know for sure. The point I'm trying to make is that I think there's something in you that's worth saving. If I didn't think this way, you can be assured that you would never have gotten up off the ground. Does that make sense? Let me put it another way. You now have one chance..." She grabbed him by his left shoulder and turned him around so that he faced her. This time he looked into Ms. Royce's eyes. "You have one chance, and how you use it will determined what happens to you next. Do you understand me? And I won't tolerate hesitation." Luke nodded his head. He wasn't confident that he could open his mouth and say anything coherent and meaningful.

"Now, let's go to the lake before it's too late. I want you to see what happens."

"What's going happen to them?"

"Who?" Ms. Royce paused. She looked directly into his eyes as if she were expecting to find something redeeming in them.

"Jimmy," Luke replied hesitantly, hoping that he had answered the question correctly and that Ms. Royce wasn't having second thoughts about helping him. "Jimmy and, I guess, his friends, although I'm not sure who all the animals are." Luke wanted to ask Ms. Royce about Iowa and the other Cygnets, but he was afraid of her answer, and he didn't want to know about all the things that happened at the lake. Turning away from Ms. Royce's eyes, Luke hung his head and silently prayed for the safety of the Cygnets and asked that Jimmy be punished severely for anything he did to them, his closest friends and his one, true family. Luke also asked for the same punishment – he realized that he was not only partly responsible for the Cygnets' fate, but he was also the source of the shame and humiliation his parents would have to bear once the word got out about what had happened this evening (and it was bound to get out, because of all the people who were here now, trying to fix the problems he caused). Luke wanted to cry, but when he glanced up at her and noticed her cold, unsympathetic expression, he held back and wiped away with the back of his sleeve the tears that were welling up at the bottoms of his eyes.

Ms. Royce didn't respond and continued to stare at him as if he hadn't said a word. When she evidently had had enough, she abruptly grabbed him by the shoulders and pulled him after her onto the path, where they walked toward the lake surrounded by large animals.

This was the very same path the Luke and the Cygnets had taken countless times to the lake, and yet it was no longer the narrow passageway between tangled trees and large outcrops of rocks that he remembered following only short time ago. It was now a broad, flattened out dirt road that was wide enough to allow large animals to walk three, sometimes four abreast. Perhaps the animals they were following had widened the path, although he couldn't help wondering if there were something more to the apparent change than he could understand or see at the moment. Regardless, the lake quickly came into view and, under the clear sky and bright moon, he could see the animals begin to leave the path and spread out among the trees and pants surrounding the lake. Once all of them – there were far too many to count – were neatly positioned like soldiers where the dogs couldn't see them, a silent order of some kind was given and all at once they began to converge slowly on the dogs, which were doing something at the edge of the water and were clearly oblivious to the presence of the other animals.

Chapter Twenty-Seven - There looked to be about ten of them

The dogs – there looked to be about ten of them, although he had trouble counting them as they frolicked around the clearing – were at times fighting over bits and pieces of something, rolling back and forth over something else, and prowling the edge, as if there was something else to be had just out of reach on the surface of the water.

The sight of Jimmy and the others filled Luke with a sickness that began in his stomach and rushed from there throughout his entire body until it came out of his mouth. He knew what had happened (there wasn't the slightest doubt), and he didn't know whether he could keep on his feet thinking about it, especially because of his own responsibility – and there was nothing that he could do to atone for his mistake, for his thoughtlessness, other than to suffer a well-merited punishment, which he was certain that Ms. Royce was devising. Even then, what had happened would stay with him in his mind, never to leave him even for a second, always lingering, always reminding him of what an animal he had become. Ultimately, he had to admit that there was nothing special about being a dog, even a lovable one, and assuming a canine form had only given him an excuse to be irresponsible, to forget about what he owed other people, and to neglect the duties that he owed his family and the Cygnets. Maybe he himself was irredeemable, he couldn't help thinking, and he suddenly felt light headed and ready to faint.

Ms. Royce, without looking at him, admonished him to keep on his feet and observe everything that was going to happen. Certain that she could divine his thoughts, Luke mustered every ounce of his strength to do what he was told, while at the same time breathing deeply and trying to keep the rest of contents of his stomach from coming up.

Jimmy abruptly wrenched something away from two other dogs that were fighting over it and ran behind the others, reveling in his triumph. The triumph was short-lived, however, for not only did the other two dogs follow him, but the other six or seven, seeing the Jimmy had something of value, turned toward him and began chasing him, nipping at his heels, and doing everything they could to claim the prize for themselves. Luke couldn't see the prize (he had his suspicions, though), but it really didn't matter because the behavior of the dogs revolted him, and he wished that he or Jimmy were the prize that the dogs were fighting over.

While he watched the murderous orgy unfold in front of him, Luke noticed that the animals -- the bears, the deer, the wolves, and all the others – had tightened their semi-circle around the edge of the lake, preventing any possibility of escape (as an added measure, they were at least three deep, which would have prevented a mouse from squeaking through). Luke was puzzled when the animals stopped instead of proceeding toward the dogs, and he was taken aback when several of them moved from one side to the other to allow a large deer to walk slowly through their midst until it was ten feet or so ahead of the rest. The deer looked exactly like the one that Ms. Royce inhabited, only it was larger and its antlers seemed almost twice as big, and the way that it commanded the attention of all the others, including Ms. Royce, suggested that it was the leader of the group.

The unexpected and commanding appearance of the deer, which had calmly and confidently strolled over to within a couple of feet of the outermost dog, quickly caught the attention of all the dogs. One by one, they stopped what they were doing when they sensed the extraordinary presence of this strange beast, and when they turned to look at it, to identify what it was that had made its presence so forcefully apparent to them, they practically froze in their tracks because of its size, firm stance, and unwavering stare. Not surprisingly, Jimmy was the last dog to become aware of the deer, although it wasn't clear to Luke whether Jimmy noticed the deer because he sensed the animal's presence or whether he noticed it because the rest of the dogs had ceased their strident noise -- barks, yelps, growls, and grunts -- and were looking intently at something behind his back. In any event, Jimmy, too, became frozen when he finally noticed the mountainous object that was eyeing them coldly, evincing not the slightest fear of their presence.

The dogs remained silent and motionless as the deer took one or two more steps closer to them. When the deer was only inches from the nearest dog (which was so struck by the larger animal's foreboding appearance that it was practically cowering), it angled its head downward so that its eyes were on the same level as the dogs' eyes, and, after two or three eruptions of snot and hot air from its nostrils, it slowly and mechanically moved its head and antlers from one dog to another, watching them even more intently, as if it were trying to memorize their faces or perhaps identify one particular dog. The animal seemed to look at Jimmy the longest, but then it moved to a couple of other dogs, and so Luke wasn't sure if there was something to its long gaze or if he was simply hoping that it had picked Jimmy out.

Obviously, Luke had no idea what would happen next. How could he? He couldn't begin to guess, in part because he couldn't tell exactly what was going on. From where he stood, he could only see the backside of the deer and some of the frightened faces of the dogs, but this was at least enough to let him know that something was going to happen to some of the dogs, most likely Jimmy.

Luke could see Jimmy clearly, however. Unlike his view of the other dogs, Luke could see everything that Jimmy did -- or, hopefully, would be done to him – because the deer had just stepped to one side and the dogs to the other, opening a visual path that led directly to his former friend. Whether this was intentional or not, he couldn't say (and it didn't matter), but it did allow him to notice something disturbing about Jimmy – the dog's jowls were frothy and stained with what looked like blood. Even in the dim light, Luke could clearly see the dark, scarlet stains, which increasingly looked like the very thing he feared the most. The visual evidence sent a shudder through him that buckled his knees and that filled him with a sense of guilt that was practically numbing. Now, he might have had some sympathy for the dogs – not that he could have forgiven them for their cruelty, even if their ruthless actions were directed against relatively insignificant animals such as mice and squirrels – but knowing what Jimmy and the others might have done to the Cygnets, Luke felt little else but revulsion and hoped that whatever was in store for them – especially for Jimmy – it would come quickly and mercilessly.

"But why don't they change back?" Luke asked Ms. Royce without turning toward her. "They're obviously afraid of the animal."

Ms. Royce glanced at him and then turned back to the scene unfolding in front of them. "Don't you know? With everything going on around them, they are only thinking like dogs, and dogs don't change into humans."

"Ever?" Luke looked at Ms. Royce.

"Not often," she replied. Keeping her eyes focused on Jimmy and the other animals, she added, "Pay attention to what's going on here."

The deer, having concluded its examination of each dog, turned and again focused its eyes on Jimmy. Having decided that he was the dog it was looking for, the deer was clearly ready for action, adjusting its huge body and sturdy shoulders so that it could position its antlers squarely on Jimmy. At that point, Luke thought, it was matter of seconds before Jimmy would meet justice. The other dogs must have noticed the same thing, and, as if they were responding to some kind of silent signal, they began to back away from Jimmy, cautiously inching toward the shadows away from the lake as a place of safety and possible escape. Jimmy wasn't completely oblivious to what was happening, however, for even if he didn't understand why the deer was focused on him, he knew that it meant business and that he needed to do something in response, quickly.

But as the seconds passed, Jimmy began to suspect that there was some hesitation in the animal (why didn't it charge?), despite its formidable appearance, and that he might actually have a chance to escape the animal or, in the best of worlds, force it to back away and maybe flee. Concentrating on the deer (he didn't dare take his eyes off the animal) and oblivious to the retreat of his friends, Jimmy was certain that if he made the right move – a move that was aggressive enough to inspire the others – the other dogs would support him and together they could easily defeat the deer (the size of the animal was nothing in comparison to the combined strength of a pack of dogs). Of course, with the animal in front of him, the lake behind him, and flat ground on both sides of him, Jimmy didn't have a lot of options to choose from, and so he decided that the only good option he had – the only option he had - - was to take the animal head on. If he were aggressive enough, if he showed the animal that he had no fear of it, then the odds for success had to be in his favor, especially if the other dogs joined him. It was brilliant.

Gently lowering his head (he didn't want to force the animal into anything before he was ready), Jimmy began growling – softly at first and then with increasing volume – and moving slowly and carefully toward the deer until he came to within six or seven feet from the animal, which throughout this time continued to stand motionless and as cold and unfeeling as an ancient statue. Pausing and eyeing the animal one last time, Jimmy suddenly started barking, loudly and frenetically like a guard dog confronting an intruder, and, in the blinking of an eye, charged the deer, heading directly toward its eyes. He was positive that the deer would either take a step back or flinch, which would enable him to attack the vulnerable areas underneath or behind the animal (bringing the others immediately to his aid) or run around the animal and escape.

Luke knew from experience that Jimmy, despite his agility, didn't stand a chance, and he was surprised that Jimmy would try something so clearly doomed to fail. Indeed, the deer was much quicker that Jimmy, and the second that Jimmy lunged for the animal, throwing his body to the right where he thought it was weakest (its left shoulder seemed slightly lower than its right), the deer's antlers were poised and ready to parry the thrust, forcing Jimmy to stop and hop back to his previous position.

The deer, however, didn't appear to want to finish off Jimmy quickly (and it was clear from its quickness and its massive body that it could do so at any second), and instead the animal merely moved its antlers with astonishing quickness as if it wanted to give Jimmy the benefit of the doubt and one chance to reconsider his actions. Or at least that's how it looked to Luke. Unfortunately, the deer's quick, decisive movements caught Jimmy off-guard and angered him, and, after he was a few feet away from the animal, he was more determined than ever to get the best of the animal and bring it down, if possible. Once more he lowered his head, although this time he was going to attack the other side, hoping that the deer was not as quick from that side. Charging again to the right (he was trying to confuse the animal), he suddenly veered and attacked on the left, hoping that the animal would become befuddled and hence vulnerable.

Just as before, however, the deer was quicker than Jimmy and had positioned its antlers to blunt the attack before Jimmy was close enough to lunge. Skidding to a stop only inches from the animal, Jimmy jumped backward several feet and, infuriated that he had failed to budge the deer so much as an inch, he careened forward again, this time intending to scramble under the antlers (he needed only a few inches) and, once beyond the antlers' reach, attack the soft wattle that hung from its neck. Confident that the animal would have trouble defending itself from this angle, Jimmy was determined to bring it down or to force it to retreat, with or without the others in pursuit.

The end was much quicker than Luke and certainly Jimmy expected. Pivoting successfully, Jimmy continued to charge with all his might, pushing to the left and lowering his body so that it would slip easily under the animal's antlers, which seemed higher that he expected. 'The animal doesn't have a clue what's happening,' Jimmy might have thought, but everything had come to a conclusion in a fraction of the time it would have taken to think it. He was within inches, maybe less, of being able to avoid the animal's antlers when with blinding speed they suddenly hit the dirt right in front of him, not only preventing him from sliding underneath but also preventing him from stopping on his own. There simply was not enough room to stop, and he slammed shoulder first into the antlers, bouncing backwards and rolling over on his side. Jimmy was dazed and unable to feel anything and, when he looked up he could tell that the impact had no effect on the animal. Before he could move another inch, though, the deer thrust its antlers downward and pinned Jimmy to the ground, forcing him onto his knees and stomach, unable to stand or even roll to his side.

Luke couldn't help wondering if this was exactly what happened to him and, for a second or two, he almost felt sorry for Jimmy, especially when he heard whines and yelps from pain and fright. His sympathy, however, probably had more in common with his own experiences than Jimmy's current problems. Thinking about what Ms. Royce had done to him, Luke watched as the deer's antlers held Jimmy to the ground, giving him absolutely no room to move, and push his nose into the soft dirt that covered the clearing, making him gag and struggle for air. The deer held firm, like the statue mentioned previously, and quite obviously didn't feel any compassion for Jimmy's plight.

Chapter Twenty-Eight - With Jimmy incapacitated

With Jimmy incapacitated and the large animals making their presence known, the other dogs quickly reverted to their human forms. "It seems that they still have a modicum of human sense," Ms. Royce mentioned to Luke, as she left his side, walked over to where they were standing, and began speaking to them. Luke could see the stern gestures she was making with her hands and arms (even the way she stood, both heels pressed together, appeared unbending and uncompromising), although he couldn't hear much of what she was saying because of the breeze that was rattling the leaves of the surrounding trees and because of the increasing din – the snorts, shakes, and coughs – coming from the animals that were becoming increasingly restless. But whatever it was, it made all the boys hang their heads and even a couple of them – Luke didn't recognize the boys – to cry. After a brief pause during which she stared down at the tops of their heads (none of the boys were looking at her), Luke thought he heard her say something like "…will be waiting for you at the park's entrance…," and something else that resembled "…don't make me come looking…" At the same time that she said these things, she pointed in that direction, which was a short distance from where they were standing. Without looking at her or anyone else, the boys left the area quietly, following the path and disappearing into the woods. Only Jimmy was left, and Luke.

Ms. Royce walked over to Jimmy, who was still imprisoned under the deer's antlers and still whimpering in pain. He was so tightly imprisoned against the ground that the only thing he could move (apart from his eyes and a small section of his nose, which was caked with mud) was his tail, and when Ms. Royce looked down at him, he wagged it feebly. It was obvious that he was asking for mercy, possibly what the other boys seemed to have been granted, but it was unlikely that Jimmy could have seen what happened to the boys as opposed to hearing it or maybe sensing their departure. Unmoved and unforgiving, Ms. Royce didn't immediately respond, and instead shook her head slightly as if to say that it would be a long time before he earned mercy and forgiveness.

The horizon was becoming lighter. The moon had disappeared, although it still gave off enough light to illuminate the tops of the trees on the far side of the lake. Birds deep in the woods were chirping and cawing, and as Luke glanced away from Ms. Royce (a vague, rustling sound drew his attention toward the trees), he noticed that the animals were turning around and walking back into the woods, disappearing as if they were figments of his imagination. Despite the increasingly lively chatter of birds and frogs somewhere among the trees, as well as the occasional crack and crash of tree branches falling from the trees (no doubt caused by the large animals slowly crashing through the woods), Luke happened to notice a familiar 'whoosh' as the lake's small waves reached the shore. Turning to take one last look at the lake, at the waters which had meant so much to him, he observed small white caps like small dashes across the water and, in the darkness at the far side of the lake, waves or debris floating on the surface of the water that resembled faint, gray exclamation points.

Luke didn't linger over the exclamation points, because he knew that Ms. Royce would be upset with him if he didn't pay attention to what she was doing. Turning back toward Ms. Royce, Luke was startled to see that she was no longer hovering over Jimmy but standing erect and facing him, Luke, her arms folded across her chest and her face cold and expressionless. Luke couldn't tell if she was expecting an answer to a question he didn't hear or silently demanding his attention. In any case, he wasn't willing to anger her, and so he straightened his posture and focused his attention on her every movement. If she had, in fact, asked him a question, he decided that it would be best to allow her to repeat the question instead of saying something stupid that would doubtless come back to haunt him. Without moving her body or her taught arms (they looked angry to Luke), she turned her head to her left and, inclining it slightly, looked down at Jimmy, who was still pathetically pinned beneath the deer's antlers, and then back at Luke. He could tell that she was indicating a relationship between him and Jimmy, and, as he looked at Jimmy, he couldn't help feeling guilt and regret for what he had done. But he felt something else as well. Looking at Jimmy, helpless, struggling for breath, and in pain, Luke again felt sorry for him. He still couldn't forgive him, but at least he was beginning to see himself in Jimmy's place – after all, it was only minutes ago that he, too, was pinned beneath a deer's antlers – and starting to understand how easy it was to succumb to thoughts and emotions that were contrary to everything he knew was right. Yes, many of the things that Jimmy did were the result of his animal nature taking control of his human nature, but that was the point, and that was at least part of the lesson that Ms. Royce was trying to teach him. If it hadn't been for Ms. Royce, he might have been in Jimmy's place. Luke wanted to close his eyes and make everything go away, to forget everything he had seen this evening, to forget Jimmy and his relationship to the boy, and to forget what happened to the Cygnets, his dearest friends in the world.

"What have I done?" Luke said to himself, while looking at Jimmy and watching him struggle for air. "If it hadn't been for me, none of this would be happening. They would still be here, they would still be Cygnets, and if they didn't like me, so what? They would still be alive." Luke began to recall some of the great times he had as a Cygnet and, especially, as a friend of Iowa. He recalled the time when they partnered for sticks, winning the game to the consternation of Press, who had accused them of cheating because they refused to battle each other, making it harder for any of the others to win. "Stinking cheater," Press had screamed, and then thought better of her anger and, laughing it off, resumed playing the game. It was a strange, meaningless memory, and yet it filled him with an intense longing for the past, for the time before Iowa's parents had died and when they all played together as if there were nothing better or more important in life. Luke relived a number of other times, each one seeming to focus on Iowa, before he again saw Jimmy, suffering for destroying the Cygnets and his, Luke's, life. Luke would have given anything to bring them back, even if they continued to despise him, even if he could never again be a Cygnet, for at least they would still be here and the Cygnet tradition would live on.

Luke noticed that Ms. Royce was no longer looking at him and, instead, was eyeing something over to his left, either in the woods or on the path. Surprised by the intensity of her gaze, Luke turned to see what had attracted her attention and observed two fairly obese people emerging from the woods carrying between them what looked like a small, nondescript box. The box, which appeared to be no more than two feet in any direction, didn't seem to be particularly heavy, although one of the individuals was having a little difficulty keeping a solid grip on a handle that protruded from its side. As they got closer to Ms. Royce, enabling Luke to see everything more clearly, he could see that it was not a box they were carrying, but a cage. The dim light had confused him, because it was now obvious that instead of walls, thin bars made up the sides and top and bottom.

The couple carrying the cage, a heavyset, middle-aged man with a heavy mustache and a shorter, slightly thinner but equally middle-aged woman, didn't say a word to Luke or even glance in his direction as they walked over to Jimmy and, after resting the cage on the ground about three feet from the deer's antlers, immediately set to work. Ms. Royce was silent, too, as she watched the couple take Jimmy's measurements with a tape measure the man had pulled from his back pocket and then compare those measurements against the cage ostensibly to make sure that the cage was the exact size for their needs. Working quickly and quietly (they hardly made a sound and, instead of speaking, would simply nod or shake a head to communicate something), displaying the speed and skill characteristic of a much younger couple, they went about their complicated business as if they had been doing this kind of work for years, as if they had done it so many times that only the rare nod or headshake was necessary to complete their business. Indeed, when it was time for the deer to lift its head and release Jimmy, the man only had to nod to the animal and wink his left eye, and it allowed enough room for the couple to reach under the sharp spikes and extract Jimmy, and they did it so quickly and efficiently that Jimmy didn't have time to lift his head or stretch his sore limbs before he had been packed into the cage, filling every inch of it so completely that only his eyes and his nostrils could move with any sort of freedom. Luke heard a couple of faint yelps in the process, but Jimmy became silent the second the man slammed the cage shut and, pulling a large key out of his other pocket, secured the door.

As soon as they were finished, the woman pulled out some papers from her purse, which amazingly had remained draped over her left shoulder during the entire process, and together they silently checked off numerous, unknown items, sometimes looking around the clearing for something before quietly agreeing that they had it or spotted it before putting their mark next to it. When they were finished (about five minutes after they had begun), the man come over to Ms. Royce and without uttering a sound presented the papers for her perusal. Ms. Royce scanned each page (there were perhaps ten pages in all, as far as Luke could tell) and, after nodding her approval, signed the last page and watched as the couple picked up Jimmy in his cage and walked down the path, disappearing into the woods.

They had been gone perhaps thirty seconds when Ms. Royce walked over to Luke and stood by his side, standing silently and looking at the deep shadows that had engulfed the strange couple. Luke wanted to know what was next, what was in store for him (would the couple come back with another cage, one for him?), but at the same time he wanted to know why Jimmy had been stuffed into such a small cage. It didn't appear merely uncomfortable; it seemed positively painful, as if they had placed him into some strange, medieval device deigned to punish him or elicit a confession. Luke had read about such devices in one of his books on ancient castles. Turning to Ms. Royce, he couldn't help asking her why Jimmy had been put into a cage, especially one so small and uncomfortable. Had the individuals misjudged the size needed?

Ms. Royce turned to him and, with a look of incredulity, asked him, "Don't you know?"

"Know what?"

"I'm amazed that you wanted to change without understanding the limitations. We don't want him to move until he reaches his destination. If he had more space, he could return to his human form, and that, of course, would ruin everything. If we don't have room to stretch out, to resume our full animal form and natural stance, then we can't become humans again and remain animals until...are you sure Iowa didn't tell you this? I'm surprised." She stared at him for a moment as if she couldn't believe that he didn't know what seemed fundamental to changing into an animal.

"Our challenge, in this case, "she resumed, "is to make sure Jimmy doesn't change back before he reaches his destination. Can you imagine what people would say if they saw your friend in a cage in the back of a truck? Seriously, if we allowed him to change, we wouldn't have a prayer of taking him where he needs to go and rehabilitating him. He would resist, and his mother would resist because all mothers have a soft spot for their children when they're in human form. It's kind of funny, isn't it? Naturally, this is a balancing act. If we keep him in his animal state too long, his human thoughts and emotions could atrophy and he might never again be able to change back, to become a human being. You weren't kidding when you said that Iowa didn't say anything about this? Anyway, if he can't change back, he would live only as long as an animal of his kind lives. How long do dogs live? Ten years? More?"

Luke didn't know if he was supposed to respond, and so he remained silent and listened carefully to Ms. Royce.

She smiled vacantly at him and then resumed her discourse. "We still have hope for Jimmy, providing we can make him understand his animal nature. He'll also have to take responsibility for his actions, but this will come in time and, of course, he'll be earning credit for working with us and learning what he is supposed to be learning. One part of this process, though, is making him understand that he must never change into an animal again. If he does that, everything that we taught him would be lost, and we might have to take sterner measures. Do you understand what I am saying? Rehabilitation isn't easy, and when you fall back after we've gone to all the trouble...well, we're not very sympathetic. It's a matter of protecting everyone. Do you see what I'm getting at here? Now, just between you and me, I suspect it's going to be a difficult process for your friend, especially at first, but if he can do everything required, he stands a good chance of making a full recovery. Do you see why I'm disappointed in Iowa?" Ms. Royce looked carefully at Luke, her eyes cold, unfeeling, animalistic.

Luke nodded his head in affirmation. He felt that she was not asking him to condemn the girl, but rather to agree to the terms of the punishment that he would have to endure. But before that happened, before he left in a cage like Jimmy, he wanted to know if his parents knew about his troubles and, if not, if Ms. Royce would be kind enough to say something to them so that they would not suffer too much over his absence. However, everything that he had just witnessed weighed so heavily on him that he couldn't speak, or at least he was certain that he couldn't utter a single word without breaking down in tears, which he knew would serve no useful purpose. Glancing around the clearing while he tried to muster some sense of self-control, Luke was surprised that everything looked as it always looked; the animals were nowhere to be seen, including the deer, and all traces of them – hoof prints, broken branches, and even the marks in the soft dirt that should have been left after the cage rested on the ground -- had all disappeared, leaving nothing behind that would have suggested that they had been here.

'When are they coming for me?' Luke asked himself, expecting the couple or someone else to return for him. He wanted to ask Ms. Royce for permission to sit down on a familiar log, since he was getting tired from the stress, but before he had a chance to open his mouth the man and woman reappeared from the darkness of the woods. Neither Jimmy nor the cage was with them. The man looked at Ms. Royce and, smiling in a slightly embarrassed manner, walked over to the spot where he had caged Jimmy and picked the key off the ground. When the woman, who had remained on the path near the entrance into the woods, saw the man pocket the key, she announced to everyone in a pleasant, almost sing-song manner that she knew he would find it there. "It would be a little troublesome without the key, I think," she added, and the two of them returned to the shadows. Luke didn't know what to make of the sudden reappearance of the couple, but there was something about them that tugged at the back of his mind. Turning to Ms. Royce for an answer, he was prevented from asking her because she seemed to have divined his thoughts.

"Yes, those are the Smiths. Their job is to rehabilitate wild animals and return them to human state. They will become Jimmy's grandparents. They're kind people, although they don't brook nonsense, especially with something as serious as this."

Luke didn't know what to say. Question after question was suddenly crowding his mind, and yet he didn't have the nerve to pepper Ms. Royce with such silly queries. Instead, the only thing he could utter was, "Iowa…"

"I'd like to hear what you understand from all this, but I realize that now is not the right time. Make an appointment with me later in the week, and we'll talk." She turned and briefly looked up at the sky. "It's getting light, and you should be going home." Ms. Royce smiled briefly in a cold way, and then turned, walked down the path, and disappeared into the woods.

Chapter Twenty-Nine - Luke was thoroughly confused

Luke was thoroughly confused by what had happened and even more so about what was now expected of him. He was certain of one thing, however – he was never again going to change into an animal. It frightened him to consider how close he had come to going wild like Jimmy, of committing crimes like Jimmy, and finally of being punished like Jimmy. Luke was willing to accept whatever punishment Ms. Royce deemed fit (and he deserved to be punished for what Jimmy did to the Cygnets), and yet he wasn't exactly eager to be put into a cage or, in fact, to begin serving his time right away.

He had taken one step to the left on his way out of the park when he decided to have one more look – for the very last time – at the lake. The sun had just crept above the horizon, sending its glorious rays into the sky and covering almost the entire surface of the lake with electric profusions of shimmering gold, yellow, and orange. Staring at the mirror-like surface of the lake (Luke shaded his eyes from areas where the reflected light was most intense), a tremor surged through his body and tears began to roll down his dirty cheeks. The Cygnets were gone, Iowa was gone, and the only remnants of their existence were the lake and his memories. But, oh, the memories would never be pleasant ones, because they would always be tinged with what had happened last night, with Jimmy's vile actions, and his, Luke's, foolish revelation. If only he had kept his mouth shut. If only Jimmy had kept his mouth shut. If only Iowa had kept the secret to herself. If only...Luke couldn't finish. He picked up a small, flat rock and threw it like a disk across the lake, where it bounced four, five, six times on the surface of the water before sinking. He recalled how he had once desired to throw a rock so hard that it would bounce from one end of the lake to another. There would be no chance of ever doing that now.

Luke was mentally and physically exhausted as he walked home, and it was all he could do to resist resting on a bench or chair in front of someone's house, or simply sitting down on the curb and hanging his head for a while. Had he any money, he would have gladly given it to lie down on someone's lawn for the rest of the day, possibly tomorrow as well. But tomorrow – Luke dreaded tomorrow, because he would have to attend classes, walk the halls, and then sit outside at lunch knowing that they would not be there – they would never be there – and he would have to listen to all the absurd suppositions regarding what had happened to Press, Lu, and Dana...and maybe even Iowa. Surely, not everyone had forgotten her. And what could he say? What was there to say? Then again, he would have to meet with Ms. Royce....he couldn't imagine how that could make things any better.

Luke had just reached the sidewalk that led to his house when a small rabbit jumped in front of him. It hesitated instead of running for cover, and for a couple of seconds it looked around as if it were confused and didn't know where it should go or where it should be. Luke couldn't help wondering if this small, troubled animal was someone he had known, someone who had been so enamored of being an animal that he had become one, never again to return to human form. Hesitating, clearly not afraid of Luke, the animal seemed like it wanted some help, a guiding hand perhaps, but it suddenly hopped away before Luke could do anything, as if it had realized who Luke was and understood the dangers of standing so close to someone who had been Jimmy's friend. It was surprising, Luke couldn't help thinking as he walked to his front door, how easy it was to succumb to one's animalistic nature, to feel so at home with one's instincts that one's heart and mind gradually eroded, making it almost impossible to return to a life in which one could control one's actions and, if that were impossible, reach out to someone like Ms. Royce for help. Reaching for the doorknob, he hesitated. He could hear his parents inside talking about something – probably the fact that he had been away for more than a day – somewhat heatedly, but not entirely angrily. They were not mad at each other (he had heard them argue enough to know the difference), and instead were directing their anger at something else…him?

Worse yet, he couldn't help fearing that Ms. Royce had already spoken to them. He dreaded that more than anything, except the problems of the previous night. But what could she have told them? That he could turn into an animal at will and that, as an animal, he had committed certain unconscionable acts? How would it affect them? Would they be able to speak to him anymore? Would their disappointment in him be such that they could no longer love him? No, Luke was certain that Ms. Royce could explain the matter in different terms, using words that conveyed the enormity of what he had done but, at the same time, allowed room for their continued love. They weren't monsters because they loved him. Maybe Ms. Royce would tell them that he had skipped school and had spent the day and night with disreputable boys (vandals, really) and did all sorts of bad things – which would be the truth and which would have the same, if not greater, effect on his parents. Luke felt sorry for his parents, for they didn't deserve this; they didn't deserve a son like him.

Opening the door and meeting his parents, Luke tried to smile and wish them a good morning (was it still morning?), but he couldn't say anything and, instead, started crying. His mother was the first to step over to him and, when she put her arm around him, the thought suddenly occurred to him that she, too, had the power to change. He couldn't exactly say why thought this, but since a good half of the town's adults seemed to be able to do this, it only made sense. Luke's father didn't take a step in any direction and, instead, crossed his arms and looked at Luke with dark, lifeless eyes.

Chapter Thirty - Simply the fear that came to her from time to time

Iowa had been scared, but her fear was simply the fear that came to her from time to time. It was the fear that all animals faced when out in the wild. Press, Lu, and Dana had not come to the lake that day. They had been so unnerved by Jimmy's attack on Press that they were beginning to rethink changing into animals. There were too many dangers, and if they spent too much time swimming around the lake, they got bored. Where was the fun in that? It was fine for Iowa, because she seemed to exist for that, but they didn't and, besides, they longed to be humans, enjoying friends and loving their families. They would never think of abandoning these things only to live a dull life in a small lake. Iowa could do that, but not them. Furthermore, it had been increasingly difficult to have fun with Iowa. She rarely wanted to be a human, and when she was a swan, she no longer seemed to care whether they played with her or went off on their own. Sometimes, she was just a swan and would have nothing to do with them in any form. They were still mad at Luke because...well, he was responsible for some of this. Maybe if he had changed into a swan, he could have prevented Jimmy from acting the way he did and possibly even controlled Iowa's worst instincts – which were those of a swan.

Maybe Iowa was ultimately responsible, but she was only a swan and truly didn't want to be anything else.

Iowa alone had been at the lake that evening, and when she sensed the arrival of the dogs, especially Jimmy, she hid beneath the trees on the other side of the lake. She knew that they might be able to scent her, but that they couldn't see her and, furthermore, she was confident that they were too stupid to come to the other side of the lake or swim out to reach her. She wasn't mistaken. The dogs did sense her presence, especially Jimmy, who kept running back and forth on the opposite edge of the lake, alternately howling and barking for the others to cross the lake and get her. Jimmy tried two or three times to swim out to her, but each time he had either become scared in the black water or had tired too quickly and realized that he needed to retreat before it became dangerous for him. The fact that they couldn't get to her – and that they knew she was there, and a great prize – drove Jimmy and a couple of the others into a frenzy, and they sought out anything that they might kill as a substitute. From her vantage point, it was hard to tell what they got, but if she was not mistaken it was a couple of rabbits, which they fought over, just like they would have fought over her.

Long before the dogs noticed Ms. Royce and the other animals, Iowa sensed their presence and their advance toward the lake. She didn't know what was happening, but she was fairly certain that their presence coincided with the presence of the dogs, not her. Still, she didn't want to show herself just in case she was mistaken, and so she maneuvered to another place at the far end of the lake that allowed her to remain in the darkest shadows while, at the same time, having a great view of the clearing and almost everything that went on there. It was all so strange. The moon illuminated the animals as they walked out of the woods, surrounding the dogs so that the only way they could escape was through the black waters of the lake. But the dogs hadn't noticed them and, like sharks, engaged in a mindless fury over bits and pieces of fur and sticks. The animals closed in, and in minutes it was all over, everyone walking home including the various humans who looked familiar but whom she couldn't place. The presence of two of the people – the Smiths – troubled her deeply and, although she didn't know why, her mind kept churning over something that she couldn't quite grasp.

The day was quiet and warm. A gentle breeze continued to blow across the lake and into the trees, creating a delicate rustle that made the lake seem especially isolated that day. Indeed, Iowa couldn't see anyone in the woods or near the lake, and despite the hush from the trees, it was quiet enough that she would have heard someone's approach from a long way away.

For the greater part of the morning, she paddled out to the center of the lake and, once there, calmly glided this way and that, occasionally scooping water over her head and back, but remaining near the center. When the sun was high overhead and the temperature warmed enough to make her sleepy and lethargic, she folded her legs beneath her, turned her head backwards and tucked it beneath her right wing, and closed her eyes, allowing herself to be gently rocked in the water and moved by the currents. Every now and then, she opened one eye (usually her left) to survey the water around her to be sure that everything was as it should be, and when that proved to be so, she closed her eye and dozed off again.

Long ago, Iowa discovered that swans dream. They don't dream like people, but they do have distinct dreams, mainly about food and floating leisurely across long expanses of water. She began dreaming this time, too, but for some reason her dreams were different, not like the kinds of dreams typical of a swan. In one instance, she thought she recognized the boy on the edge of the water, whose head hung low and who appeared to be hurt or injured (why else would he hang his head?). In another instance, she thought she recognized the people carrying the strange object that had swallowed the dog. This dream, the recognition of the people, sent long tendrils of fear coursing through her body, and she woke up with a start. She looked around and, seeing nothing amiss, went back to sleep.

In her final dream, she could see the woman with freckles across her nose smiling at her and patting her neck. Iowa must have been hurt, because the woman kept repeating, "It's okay, it's okay." Iowa recognized the woman, or at least she thought she did, but for some reason she couldn't recall any particulars of why she recognized her and what importance she may have had in her life. This was the very woman, she realized a moment later, who had stood by the young boy with the injured neck, and she continued to pet Iowa and coo. "It's okay, no one is going to hurt you." The sound of her voice – it was quiet and gentle – and the manner in which she articulated her words – it was as if she truly had control over the outcome of things she was promising would be fine. For the first time in what seemed like years, Iowa felt completely at ease and secure, especially when the woman continued to say that things were okay and that nothing was going to hurt her.

"It's okay, no one's going to hurt you," the voice said again, and Iowa opened her eyes to see if the woman was there, possibly reaching out to stroke Iowa on the head or the back. At first, things were a blur through one eye, and then as she opened both eyes and looked around, she didn't see the woman and, instead, noticed a strange haze descending on her and, outside of the haze, a couple of young human boys on either side and approaching within inches of her. Within a second, the boys were on top of her, holding her neck and wings tightly to her body.

www.ingramcontent.com/pod-product-compliance
Lightning Source LLC
Chambersburg PA
CBHW061552170626
46811CB00001B/174